Samuel French Acting Edition

Kind Lady

by Edward Chodorov

I0589016

|| SAMUEL FRENCH ||

SAMUELFRENCH.COM   SAMUELFRENCH.CO.UK

FOR PRODUCTION ENQUIRIES

UNITED STATES AND CANADA
Info@SamuelFrench.com
1-866-598-8449

UNITED KINGDOM AND EUROPE
Plays@SamuelFrench.co.uk
020-7255-4302

Each title is subject to availability from Samuel French, depending upon country of performance. Please be aware that KIND LADY may not be licensed by Samuel French in your territory. Professional and amateur producers should contact the nearest Samuel French office or licensing partner to verify availability.

Please refer to page 139 for further copyright information.

"KIND LADY" was first presented by H. C. Potter and George Haight at the Booth Theatre in New York City, Tuesday evening, April 23, 1935. The play was staged by Mr. Potter, the setting was designed by Jo Mielziner and the cast was as follows:

MR. FOSTER ....Played by		*Francis Compton*
MARY HERRIES	" "	*Grace George*
LUCY WESTON	" "	*Irby Marshal*
ROSE	" "	*Marie Paxton*
PHYLLIS GLENNING	" "	*Florence Britton*
PETER SANTARD	" "	*Alan Bunce*
HENRY ABBOTT	" "	*Henry Daniell*
ADA	" "	*Justine Chase*
DOCTOR	" "	*Alfred Rowe*
MR. EDWARDS	" "	*Thomas Chalmers*
MRS. EDWARDS	" "	*Elfrida Derwent*
AGGIE EDWARDS	" "	*Barbara Shields*
GUSTAV ROSENBERG	" *	*Jules Epailly*

SCENES

PROLOGUE

An Afternoon in Spring.

ACT ONE

Scene 1—Late Christmas Eve several years before.
Scene 2—After dinner the following January.

ACT TWO

An afternoon later in January.

ACT THREE

An afternoon the following summer.

EPILOGUE

The action of the play takes place in the living room of Mary Herries' home in Montague Square, London.

SCENE

The downstairs living room in Mary Herries' house in Montague Square, London.

The room proper is a large, comfortably furnished living room reflecting the excellent taste and character of Mary Herries. Many of its furnishings, the pictures in particular, are objets d'art. In the Right wall are two large casement windows with fine lace curtains and heavy drapes. In the Left wall is a large fireplace (downstage) and a door (upstage) leading to the dining room. Above the mantel is a large oil painting, a Whistler.

Up Center is a large arch. Going upstage through the arch one rises two steps to a platform that extends off Right to the front hall and door, and off Left to the rear of the house. Up stage of the platform two more steps lead to a bay window, and stair landing. Leading Left from this bay-window landing is a flight of stairs to the upper part of the house.

Between the windows at Right is a desk and chair. A sofa with a coffee table in front of it is at Right. Against the Right section of the back wall is a chest and in the up Right corner is a table with a lamp.

In front of the fireplace is a low upholstered fire seat. Two large over-stuffed chairs with a drum table between them occupy the Left side of the stage.

Against the Left side of the back wall is a chest and at its Right is a low table with a lamp. On the wall above these are an El Greco, and a Whistler. Above the furniture at up Right on the back wall are two more Whistlers.

Between the windows in the bay window is a large chest. The windows have drapes and curtains.

A chandelier hangs in the hall and there are wall brackets at Right and Left on the pilasters framing the big Center arch.

PROLOGUE

Scene: There is a slight rearrangement of furniture on stage Right. The sofa is between the windows Right with the coffee table below it. The desk is Right with a side chair behind it and another side chair at its Left.

On the Right and Left back walls and over the fireplace the "old masters" have been replaced by "moderns."

At Rise: Empty stage. It is raining outside. It is late afternoon.

After the curtain rises the doorbell is heard ringing. After a moment it rings again. A SERVANT *is seen crossing on the platform above the Center arch from the rear of the house* (Left) *toward the front door* (Right). *The doorbell rings again.*

MR. FOSTER. [*Off.*] Mr. Abbott, please.

SERVANT. [*Off.*] Mr. Abbott's out.

FOSTER. [*Entering to Center of platform. He is a small man. He carries an umbrella, hat and brown paper envelope, and wears a coat.*] I'm from the bank, Foster's the name. I had an appointment for four o'clock. [SERVANT *gestures him to sit down and wait.*] Then, if you don't mind, I'll take off my coat—it's damp.

3

[FOSTER *removes his coat, gives it, his hat and umbrella to* SERVANT *who exits Right and after leaving them crosses out Left.* FOSTER *in the meantime has come down into the room proper. Gone to the Left end of the desk and left his envelope there. He then crosses Right, glances out the window and then at the pictures. His attention is drawn to someone coming down the stairs. It is* MARY HERRIES. MARY HERRIES *comes down from upstairs uncertainly and rather furtively. She steps on the platform and looks off Left. She turns and starts off Right on the platform.*]

FOSTER. [*Stopping her as she reaches the Center of the platform.*] How do you do? [MARY *stops but doesn't answer.*] I am waiting for Mr. Abbott, if you please, Madam. I'm from the bank. I have an appointment for four o'clock, but since he's not here, perhaps—

MARY. Mr. Abbott—is—not here?

FOSTER. No. Servant said he was out. Perhaps I should come back later.

MARY. [*Crossing on platform and looking off Left.*] They—don't usually keep people waiting.

FOSTER. That's all right. I don't mind waiting. Only I hope I'm not in the way.

MARY. [*Crossing down Center off platform.*] No. You're not in the way. Of course not— From the bank?

FOSTER. [*Still at Right of desk.*] Blakely's, Madam.

MARY. Oh, yes. I know that bank very well. I used to do business with Blakely's Bank.

FOSTER. [*Crossing down Right to in front of desk.*] Excuse me, Madam.—But is there any possibility that Mr. Abbott may not be here shortly? I'm to see another gentleman at five.

MARY. You've never been here before?

FOSTER. No, Madam.

MARY. Then you've never seen me before. I don't see many people—from outside.

FOSTER. Oh.

MARY. Don't you think it odd that I never see anyone?

FOSTER. Why—I don't know, Mrs.—

MARY. Miss—Mary Herries.

FOSTER. Oh. [*Then suddenly.*] Herries? It seems to me I remember the name, Madam. It's been on our books for years.

MARY. Yes— It has been. For years.

FOSTER. But I thought—I mean I took it for granted—that you were away. Abroad, or some place. For several years, I think?

MARY. No, I've been here—always. [MARY *crosses above to dining room door and closes it. Then comes back to* FOSTER *who has come to Center.*] Don't you want to know why I never see anyone?

FOSTER. Uh—what is that, Madam?

MARY. It's a very interesting reason. Very interesting. I

think you might be very interested. You might be the very one.

[*During this last speech the lights have been slowly fading—and at the end of the speech the stage is in total darkness.*]

ACT ONE

Scene I

The lights fade up very shortly and we find the stage is set as first described.

LUCY WESTON *is discovered sitting in the chair Left in front of the fireplace. In the chair Left Center is an open suitcase with wrapped Christmas packages in it. There are also some packages on the table Left and an envelope.*

It is late Christmas Eve, several years before the Prologue. A small Christmas tree is on the chest in the bay window.

ROSE. [*Entering immediately after the lights are up with a piece of red ribbon and a tray containing a whiskey decanter, syphon, and glasses.*] This is all I could find, Mrs. Weston.

[ROSE *puts tray on chest Upper Left and crosses to table Left and ties up a Christmas package.*]

LUCY. Fine! That will do nicely. Now let me see. Cynthia, Peter, John, Harold, Kitten and Sybil. That's seven. Seven nieces and nephews. Rose, think of it. And I didn't have to go through a thing to have them! It is quite different when I have my own chickabiddies.

ROSE. Oh—Mrs. Weston!

LUCY. What's this? [*She notices a package which hasn't been put in suitcase.*] "Rose." Now who in heaven's name! Has my brother had another child? I mean his wife? Dear me it's hard to keep track, Rose— [*Looks at* ROSE.] Oh, my heavens! It's *you!* I nearly packed it with the others. Well, now the cat's out of the bag. [*Hands package to* ROSE.] Merry Christmas, Rose.

ROSE. [*Crossing in front of table.*] Oh, thank you, Mrs. Weston. The same to you and many more.

LUCY. Well—we won't count how many more. And— [*Takes envelope.*] This. For looking after me so nicely this visit.

ROSE. [*Takes envelope.*] Oh, Mrs. Weston. This is too much!

LUCY. When you open it you won't say that. Well, things are going to get better some day. Those go in the bag to take with me tomorrow. Don't let me forget. Am I all packed?

ROSE. [*Putting packages in suitcase.*] Yes, Madam. Except for the blouse at the cleaner's. I'll send that on to you the moment it comes.

LUCY. That's fine. What time is it?

ROSE. [*Puts suitcase on floor above table.*] After eleven o'clock, Madam.

LUCY. What time are these operas usually over, Rose.

ROSE. [*Straightens Left Center chair.*] It's hard to say

Mrs. Weston. But Miss Herries always leaves early when the weather's bad.

LUCY. There's one place I will not be found on Christmas Eve— And that is an opera house. Well—I have to leave in half an hour. Miss Herries is sure to be back by then, isn't she?

ROSE. [*Going upstairs.*] That's hard to say, Mrs. Weston.

[*Front doorbell rings.* ROSE *puts suitcase on landing Right and goes to answer it.*]

PHYLLIS. [*Off stage.*] Is Miss Herries in?

ROSE. [*Off stage.*] No, Miss, she's not back from the Opera.

[PHYLLIS *enters and stops at Center on platform.*]

PHYLLIS. Oh, dear, I was sure she'd be here. [*Sees* LUCY.] Mrs. Weston! Merry Christmas.

LUCY. Hello, Phyllis, Merry Christmas!

PHYLLIS. I'm doing the rounds of the relatives, bearing gifts. [ROSE *picks up suitcase and is crossing toward stairs.* PHYLLIS *turns toward off Right.*] Peter! Come in—don't stand out there in the hall. [*To* ROSE.] Don't go, please. [ROSE *stops at foot of stairs.* PHYLLIS *calling off Right.*] Peter!

PETER. [*Off.*] Huh?

LUCY. [*Confidentially.*] Is this—

PHYLLIS. I don't know yet, but I think so. [PETER *en-*

ters, carrying small package.] Peter, this is Mrs. Weston. Mrs. Weston, Mr. Santard. [*Takes package.*]

PETER. [*Crosses to Upper Right Center.*] How do you do?

LUCY. How do you do?

PHYLLIS. Please put this—by the tree tomorrow morning. [*Gives* ROSE *package.*]

ROSE. Yes, Miss. [*Exits upstairs.*]

PHYLLIS. Peter's an American.

PETER. You know—

[*Acknowledging this,* PETER *gives slight Indian war cry.*]

PHYLLIS. Now Peter, not *that* American!

PETER. Sorry.

PHYLLIS. Say something nice, Peter.

PETER. [*To* MRS. WESTON.] Are you Aunt Mary?

LUCY. No, I'm just—visiting—Phyllis' Aunt Mary.

PETER. I've heard a great deal about Aunt Mary and—
[*Brightly, for* PHYLLIS' *benefit.*] I've wanted to meet her! [*Nods to Phyllis with a "How's that?" expression.*]

PHYLLIS. [*Crosses off platform to Upper Center.*] You see—Peter and I—thought it would be a good idea to *bring* Aunt Mary her present—and now she isn't here! Peter!

PETER. [*Who has been looking around the room.*] Oh! How do you like London, Mrs. Weston?

LUCY. Why—I should be asking that of you!

PETER. I know—that's why I asked you first.

PHYLLIS. Don't mind Peter, Mrs. Weston. No one in New York would dream of giving him a job so his father sent him over here!

LUCY. I think he's very charming. Sit down, and tell me about— [*Sees decanter.*] Oh, would you like a drink?

PETER. Yes, please—and *no* ice.

PHYLLIS. No, Peter. No time.

PETER. [*Bowing politely to* LUCY.] Merry Christmas.

[*Crosses up onto platform at Right.*]

PHYLLIS. Sorry, Mrs. Weston. We have miles and miles of driving to do. [*Telephone.*] Good night.

LUCY. Good night. [*Crossing toward telephone on desk Right.*]

PETER. [*Going off Right.*] Goodbye.

[ROSE *enters down the stairs.*]

PHYLLIS. Don't tell Aunt Mary we were here. Present —secret. Merry Christmas.

[*Exits Right—followed by* ROSE.]

LUCY. Merry Christmas, Phyllis. [*At telephone.*] Hello? Hello, Bunny! I'm on my way! Really I am—I thought I might induce Mary Herries to "step out" this once—

What do you mean she's "no fun"?—Of course you don't know her— The car?— Oh, lovely— Yes—half an hour. Right you are. [*Hangs up.*]

PHYLLIS. [*Off.*] Merry Christmas.

ROSE. [*Off.*] Merry Christmas, Miss.

[ROSE *enters from Right. Crosses and Exits door Left to dining room.* LUCY *crosses above sofa toward Center as* ROSE *enters from dining room with a plate of sandwiches on a tray.*]

LUCY. Oh, those look good! [ROSE, *about to put sandwiches on table Left comes to* LUCY *at Upper Center and offers them.*] Er—no. Not until I'm down ten more pounds. [*Turns away but looks back at sandwiches.*] Oh, well. Christmas comes but once a year. [*Takes a sandwich.*] Thank you. [*Crosses and sits Left end of sofa.*]

ROSE. [*Putting sandwiches on table Left.*] Is there anything else, Madam?

LUCY. No – except my trunk. I'm sure I'll be in no mood tomorrow to worry about that.

ROSE. [*Takes whiskey and syphon from chest Upper Left and puts on table Left.*] The baggage people promised to be here at seven sharp they said.

LUCY. Well, if they're pretty and have curly hair you wake me up, Rose. Otherwise I'll leave their money on the dressing table.

ROSE. [*Laughs.*] Yes, Madam. [*Exits to dining room.*]

[*The door is heard to open and* MARY HERRIES *enters.*]

MARY. [*In arch.*] Hello! Head better, dear? [*Rings bell Left of arch for* ROSE.]

LUCY. Much.

MARY. Good! [*Speaking off Right.*] Come in. [HENRY ABBOTT *appears and crosses to Upper Right Center. He is tall, handsome, emanates strength and charm immediately. Shabbily, miserably dressed.*] Here's a hungry young man we've got to feed, Lucy.

HENRY. [*Very quietly, half smiling.*] Just a cup of tea, thanks.

MARY. Oh, nonsense.—You've made me take you in here at this time of night. You'll have to justify it.

HENRY. I'm afraid I couldn't manage much more.—

[ROSE *enters from dining room to above chair Left Center.*]

MARY. Rose, would you make some tea, and let this gentleman have anything else he wants.—[*To* HENRY.] If you feel better.

HENRY. Just some tea.

[*There is a moment's pause.*]

ROSE. [*Who has been eyeing him, crosses to platform Left.*] This way, please. [*He turns and follows* ROSE *out Left past arch without any further sign.*]

MARY. [*Crossing Left, puts purse on table Left.*] Poor chap.

LUCY. Where did you find him?

MARY. [*Crosses to Center.*] Just outside—I've never done this before! I never even give— [*Crossing to desk Right.*] to beggars on the street. Anyway, all I had was a one pound note.—[*Reflects.*] There's something about him.—Don't you think? [*Puts wrap on desk chair.*]

LUCY. Mmm.—

MARY. Matter of fact.—Made me feel awfully sorry for him. I just couldn't leave him standing there.—But I'd never have brought him in if you weren't here. [*Laughs.*] Haven't I been trying to convince you that I'm getting sillier all the time! I really should apologize! [*Crosses Center.*]

LUCY. [*Taking a cigarette.*] What for?

MARY. After all, heavens *what* he is.

LUCY. What he looks like probably—a rather charming, hungry young man.—

MARY. Isn't he?—Striking, I mean.

LUCY. Very.

MARY. So unusual.—

LUCY. Very.—How was Covent Garden?

MARY. [*Above table Left taking off gloves.*] Horrible I thought.—The place reeked of mackintoshes and galoshes. I could see the strings resenting it bitterly. I hate London at this time of year.

LUCY. In a few weeks I'll be home—in my garden— with an armful of the loveliest azaleas *you* ever saw.

MARY. What a persistent woman!—Oh, I feel so stupid refusing.

LUCY. Well now, why refuse? Now look here! Why shouldn't you give yourself a month of Riviera sun and warmth? What's keeping you here?

MARY. I don't know.—It's simply—

LUCY. Simply rot.

MARY. Lucy, I'd love to go back with you.—

LUCY. Then why not?

MARY. But I'm just comfortable here, I suppose—

LUCY. Why do you avoid everyone?

MARY. [*Not listening and looking off Left.*] You know, Lucy, he didn't ask me for money.

LUCY. What???—Ohh.

MARY. He simply stood there with the most disarming smile and said: "I wonder if I might have a cup of tea on Christmas Eve."—

LUCY. Very touching.—I asked you why you avoid everyone.

MARY. [*Crosses to Left Center chair and sits.*] I? I don't do anything of the sort. I've just been busy—that's all.

LUCY. Don't tell me, Mary Herries. Won't you come with me tonight, just this once? Bunny would love to have you. [*Crosses Center.*]

MARY. No, thank you, Lucy.

LUCY. Oh, ho! You're going to have a nice little chat with Tiny Tim.

MARY. Who?

LUCY. The striking young beggar you met in the fog—or snow—on Christmas Eve.

MARY. I am not! When he's had something to eat, Rose can let him out through the basement.

LUCY. Aren't you going to give him some money or something?

MARY. No, I am not.

LUCY. At least you must let him thank you.

MARY. Not necessarily.

LUCY. Well—if you want to sit all alone on Christmas Eve—I'll stay with you. I'll ring up Bunny. [*Starts Right.*]

MARY. [*Rises and crosses to* LUCY.] No, Lucy. I won't let you. Please go and have a good time.

[ROSE *enters from Left on platform.*]

ROSE. He's finished, Madam.

MARY. [*Turns to* ROSE.] What?

ROSE. He's had his tea.

MARY. [*Up Center.*] Very well, Rose. You can show him out downstairs.

ROSE. But— [*She pauses.*]

MARY. Yes—?

ROSE. He says he wants to thank you.

LUCY. [*Right Center.*] There!

MARY. That's very nice of him. Tell him he's quite welcome.

LUCY. Mary!

ROSE. Yes, Miss Herries.

[*Turns to go—but* HENRY *enters from Left on platform, crosses to Upper Left Center.*]

HENRY. [*Half smiling; a peculiar sombre smile.*] I've had my tea. You're very kind.

MARY. I was happy to help you.

HENRY. I wanted to thank you, that's all.

MARY. Of course.

[*There is a pause.*]

HENRY. [*Sees sandwiches on table Left.*] I—I wonder if I might take a few of those sandwiches.

LUCY. [*Ill at ease.*] Please do!

MARY. Of course.

HENRY. [*Crosses to table Left.*] I'll eat them outside.

[*Doorbell.* ROSE *goes Right.*]

LUCY. [*Mischievously.*] Eat them here!

[MARY *looks uncomfortably at* LUCY.]

HENRY. Thank you. I'm able to now, I think. [*Looks at whiskey.*]

MARY. [*Weakly.*] Have some whiskey if you like.

HENRY. I will.

[ROSE *enters.* HENRY *crosses below table Left and mixes whiskey and soda.*]

ROSE. The car's at the door for Mrs. Weston. [*Exits Right.*]

LUCY. Oh, dear! Well— [*Mischievously.*] Good night, Mary, and—A Merry Christmas.

MARY. Merry Christmas, Lucy. I'll see you in the morning.

LUCY. I hope so. [*She goes Right.*]

HENRY. [*Looking at paintings.*] You've a few nice things here.—[MARY *smiles nervously—looking covertly back over her shoulder for* ROSE.] That's a good El Greco. [*Points to Upper Left back wall.*]

MARY. [*Indicates immediately she is quite astonished.*] It's not bad.—

HENRY. [*Crossing Up Left.*] One of his early ones; they're not common.

MARY. [*At Upper Center.*] No.—There aren't two hundred people in London who'd know that! Are you an artist?

HENRY. Not really. One of many confused talents.

MARY. You talk as if you knew something about painting.

HENRY. I suppose I do. [*He starts toward sandwiches.*]

MARY. Look here—if you really want something to eat now—those stale sandwiches— [*Paces to chair Left Center.*]

HENRY. They're exactly right.—Again thanks. And again forgive me for disturbing you like this.

[ROSE *enters and gets* MARY'S *wrap at desk.*]

MARY. You haven't. It isn't every day one bumps into an El Greco lover on the street.

[ROSE *exits Left on platform, a bit uneasy.*]

HENRY. [*Looking around again, crosses Left.*] You collect seriously.—

MARY. [*Amused.*] How do you tell? Is this room that bad?

HENRY. [*Quickly—crossing Up Left and pointing.*] It's lovely of course.—But it takes a collector to jam a Whistler, an El Greco, and a Ming horse all together, doesn't it?

MARY. [*After a moment.*] Well, whatever you are, you have an educated eye—no question about that! And you're right about the jam.—[*Carries horse from Upper Left chest and puts it on Upper Right chest.*] There seems to be a difference between my maid and myself as to just where this bronze belongs!

HENRY. Your maid is a strong-minded woman.

MARY. [*Laughs—crossing Down Right.*] You've found that out?—Rose is a good soul—and devoted to me. She won't go to bed now until she's quite sure you don't mean to murder me.—[*Sits Right end of sofa,* HENRY *laughs and drinks.*] What do you do?

HENRY. [*Crossing to Center.*] Nothing. Everything. The last year I've had odd jobs I shouldn't like to mention in this house.—[*Crosses to sofa, puts glass on table below sofa.*]

MARY. But you certainly have a good eye—and knowledge. Collecting *is* my one interest.

HENRY. Mine, too, once—and not wasted. [*Sits Left end of couch.*] I find it very comforting to remember, standing in the line on the embankment.

MARY. The line?

HENRY. The bread line.—

MARY. Oh.—

HENRY. As a connoisseur of lines—I should say it was the best in London—and wonderfully philanthropic. I bothered you tonight because the two odd miles to the embankment seemed to stretch like eternity in the snow.

MARY. I'm glad you did.

HENRY. I, too.

MARY. [*Pause.*] Are you alone?

HENRY. Alone, as they say, in the world?

MARY. Yes.

HENRY. Practically. I have a wife—and a child.

MARY. Oh—really?

HENRY. A nursing child.

MARY. [*Very sympathetically.*] What do you do?

HENRY. We do rather nicely comparatively. Ada—my wife—is a delicate creature who scrubs floors occasionally, when she's lucky, in an office building in the City—a Fragonard charwoman.

MARY. A nursing child.—That's dreadful.

HENRY. Not at all. What Ada makes pays the rent of our hovel in South Wharf Road—and buys approximately enough food for herself and the little brute, of course.

MARY. South Wharf Road. You live—

HENRY. In the neighborhood.—I've admired the outside of your house many times—from the drinking trough opposite. [*Pointing off Right.*]

MARY. [*Rises, crosses Center.*] And I'm going to send you back to your house right now.

HENRY. [*Rises.*] Of course—I'm keeping you up.—

MARY. That's an unkind remark, young man. I could sit here and tell you how I got that El Greco until you beg for mercy. But I won't—for a very good reason [*Starts Up Center.*]

HENRY. [*Stopping her.*] I should like to hear.—

MARY. Oh, no. [*Turns back to* HENRY *at Center.*] All my life the mistakes that I've made—and there have been plenty—have all arisen from the same thing—my heart swamping my good sense. [*She looks at him. Paces to* HENRY.] I'm telling you this because you're obviously a very unusual and intelligent young man— and you've just told me a terribly pathetic story.

HENRY. [*Smiling.*] Thank you. I'm sorry.—

MARY. I'm afraid of it—and you.—I had a birthday a short time ago, and I thought at last I'm too old to be foolish any more. But here I am—helping an entirely unknown man into my house in the middle of the night and listening to a tale that's going to make me see white-faced babies in my dreams for a week.

HENRY. He's red as a herring—and looks like one.

MARY. Believe me—I don't care. Everything about you conspires to make me help you. Why—you even live around the corner! Well, I'm not going to help you. I'm a selfish old maid—and I never want to see you again— or hear anything more about that young girl you've presented with a baby. You're probably the worst sort of criminal.—[*Turns and goes to Upper Center, as she finishes speech, then turns back quickly.*] Wait a minute.—[*Goes upstairs and off.*]

[HENRY *looks after her quietly. Finishes whiskey and puts glass on table below sofa. Then slowly crosses Left and easily he picks up a white jade cigarette case from table, examines it, takes out cigarette, taps it against the case, looks at case again, then puts it in his pocket in the most natural manner in the world—as if it had come*

*from there. He lights his cigarette, crossing to below
couch. As* MARY *comes down carrying a heavy cloth
coat with a fur collar, over her arm,* HENRY *puts out
cigarette.*]

MARY. [*Hands him coat.*] Give this to your wife.

HENRY. That's good of you.

MARY. [*Going on as she gets her purse from table
Left.*] She'd better let a tailor do the alterations. Here.
—[HENRY *crosses to her.*] And you'd better get some
shoes.

HENRY. [*Without the slightest emotion.*] You're sav-
ing our lives.

MARY. Nonsense.—[*He looks at the money in his hand.*]
It's all I have in the house—so you needn't bother holding me up now, you see?

HENRY. It *was* foolish of you to let a tramp in here at
this time of night.

MARY. So I've been told. But an old woman like me—
what's the difference?

HENRY. I could have cut your throat.

MARY. You might have—but you'd have been sorry.

HENRY. Oh, no. The police never catch anybody any
more.

MARY. [*Going to arch Right and onto platform.*] Don't
let's worry about that.

HENRY. Not tonight.—It would be ungrateful.—

MARY. Goodbye.

[HENRY *crosses to Right of* MARY *on platform—turns to her.*]

HENRY. Good night. [*Exits Right.*]

MARY. [*Calling off.*] Good luck. And—Merry Christmas!

[MARY *comes in. Hesitates in arch. Goes to above chair Lower Center, looks for cigarette case on table, then on chest Up Left. Then on mantel.*]

ROSE. [*Enters from Left, stays on platform Left.*] Is there anything you want, Madam?

MARY. [*Looks for cigarette case.*] No, Rose. You can go to bed.

ROSE. Yes, Madam— Good night. [*Starts to go Left.*]

MARY. Rose.—Have you seen my cigarette case?

ROSE. [*Comes to table Left.*] The white jade, Madam? [MARY *nods.*] It was layin' right there this evening.

MARY. I thought so. [*Pause as they both reflect about* HENRY.] Oh, well—never mind.

ROSE. I'd say he took it, Madam.

MARY. Oh, no, Rose.

ROSE. Do you know where to find him, Madam?

MARY. Mmmmm.—It doesn't matter.

ROSE. Oh, dear—that's too bad.—[*Puts stopper in decanter on table Left.*]

MARY. No, Rose—he didn't take it—I remember now
—I had it with me in the taxi.

ROSE. I didn't like him at all, Madam. Too good-lookin'.

MARY. [*Sits chair Left.*] He was good-looking, wasn't
he?

ROSE. Too much so— I don't believe he was hungry
at all. The way he sat in the kitchen!—You're not
hungry, I said to myself—you're too good-looking.
—And you're up to something. And sure enough.
[*Picks up sandwich plate—crosses toward sofa.*]

MARY. No, Rose. [ROSE *stops and turns to* MARY.] I left
it in the taxi, I'm sure.

ROSE. [*Shaking her head.*] Yes, Madam.—[*Picks up
glass from coffee table and goes to dining room door.*]
Good night. [*Exits.*]

[*Christmas chimes from a church ring out.* MARY
*doesn't answer. Looks toward arch Right. Turns front
— shrugs shoulders.*]

CURTAIN

ACT ONE

Scene II

Night—Two weeks later, January.
PHYLLIS *sitting on couch reading.* PETER
*standing in front of Troubetzkoi on table
Left with glass.* PETER *looks at Troubetzkoi
for a pause.* PETER *walks away about three
steps Right, half-looking at Troubetzkoi,
then stops, returns to statue, looks at it
again.* PETER *puts glass down deliberately on
table. Takes out match, strikes it and holds
it to statue.*

PHYLLIS. Peter! Peter, put those matches away and sit
down.

[PETER *hastily shakes out match and picks up brandy
glass.*]

PETER. [*Indicates Troubetzkoi.*] That—is a woman.
—Phyllis! We must get one of those.

PHYLLIS. Yes, dear.

[*Looking at her,* PETER *walks imitating a tight-rope
walker, toward stage Right. He stops in front of picture
—looks at it for a pause—then suddenly—with extreme
deliberation, he puts his glass down on chest Upper
Right.*]

PHYLLIS. Peter, *please* don't set off any more matches!

[PETER *picks up glass and comes Center.*]

PETER. Phyllis—who's that tall thin girl last night with the— [*Makes series of adenoidal noises saying:*] "So pleased to meet you so very nice"—can't understand a word she says—who *is* that?

PHYLLIS. That, my dear—will be your cousin Elizabeth.

[PETER *looks at her for a moment.*]

PETER. That'll be nice.—And *who*—was the fat gentleman with the— [*Indicates fat stomach.*] and—the— [*Indicates pompous look and monocle.*]

PHYLLIS. [*Cuts in.*] If you're attempting to describe Sir Arthur Verne—he's a *very* dear friend of Mother's —and happens to be a *very* distinguished man.

PETER. [*Agreeing quickly.*] Yes—yes, indeed—I could see that.—[*Suddenly gets a glint in his eyes and goes into the next speech as though he were tremendously puzzled.*] But who—*who*—was the little feller! [*He extends his hand about chest high.*]

PHYLLIS. Who?

PETER. You know— [*Drops his hand about a foot.*] The *little* feller.

PHYLLIS. What are you talking about?

PETER. [*Drops his hand to about a foot from the floor —bending way over—and holding this stance. Speaks patiently.*] The *little* feller!—with the— [*Lifts his hand to pull at his chin.*]

PHYLLIS. With the *what*—

PETER. The goatee!

PHYLLIS. Peter—get *up!*

PETER. [*Straightens.*] But who *is* he? Really!

PHYLLIS. There's no one like that in our family.

PETER. No? [*He shudders.*]

PHYLLIS. No.

PETER. Funny.—I keep seeing him everywhere.—

PHYLLIS. Peter, you simply mustn't drink brandy.

PETER. There's only *one* of your family that I really like.

PHYLLIS. Really?

PETER. [*Pointing wisely upstairs.*] Aunt Mary.—

PHYLLIS. [*Rises and crosses Right behind sofa.*] We are rude, Peter, but we simply must dash off!

PETER. [*Sitting sofa Left.*] Well, let's not! Let's stay here instead.

PHYLLIS. [*With mock weariness, but real annoyance.*] Darling—how can we?

PETER. I feel mellow and witty and dignified all at once for the first time in my life! I don't want to go out in the cold world!

PHYLLIS. [*Patronizingly crossing Center.*] It has been awfully nice—but you have no sense of responsibility

PETER. I like it here! This is what I call gracious living and it's the first dinner party I've enjoyed in a long while.

PHYLLIS. Much as you hate doing the rounds, you've simply *got* to. I don't like these continual introductions either. But do you make it any easier for me? No! You act as though I were whipping you through hoops **or** something!

PETER. Can't stand being introduced—wholesale.

PHYLLIS. You spend most of the time standing around and grinning foolishly at everyone.

PETER. I'm not grinning foolishly now. I like Miss Herries—and I'm crazy about this house—and I hope that— [*Closes his eyes.*] the solidification—of our relationship will permit me to run in and out of here at frequent intervals. [*Both laugh.*] Furthermore, she has the best wine I ever tasted. [*He reaches for brandy decanter.*]

PHYLLIS. [*Taking his glass out of his hand and crossing and putting it table Left.*] Don't imagine you can pop in and out of here whenever you please!

PETER. [*Lighting cigarette.*] Why not?

PHYLLIS. Aunt Mary isn't a very sociably inclined lady.

PETER. She's damn nice.

PHYLLIS. [*Above table Left.*] I know. We must see her more often, really. Most of the family don't, you know.

PETER. I'll see her without the family any time.

PHYLLIS. We've all neglected her shamefully.

PETER. Your dear mother.

PHYLLIS. Oh, no—it's not Mother. She couldn't keep me away. I don't know why—I'm so horribly busy.

PETER. Trotting me around to meet cousins and uncles.

PHYLLIS. [*Crosses to Center.*] I hope she doesn't think this was that kind of a duty call. [*Crossing Up Center.*] Wonder what she's doing?

PETER. You hinted strongly enough that a wedding present would be acceptable.

PHYLLIS. [*Crossing Down Center.*] Now, Peter, that's not done.

PETER. Maybe she's gone to get us a present right now.

PHYLLIS. How many times must I tell you that I'm not showing you off to my relations just to get presents from them?

PETER. Then why visit the Howards tonight? Why not stay here awhile?

PHYLLIS. George Howard's not a relative. He's your best client— [*Crossing in front of sofa to Right.*] Or will be now that he knows you're going to marry me.

PETER. I feel as if I were getting married for business reasons.

PHYLLIS. Marriage *is* a business.

PETER. Yeah!

PHYLLIS. Yes!

PETER. I suppose I'll go to the Howards whether I want to or not. And all the other places. [*Rises and turns to* PHYLLIS.] "How do you do? Yes—I'm the lucky fellow! When! Oh, about the first of June. Yes! The first of June. What? Oh, I'm an American bond salesman. Do you want any nice bonds so I can get married?"

PHYLLIS. Ok.! "I want you to meet Peter. I met him in New York, but he's over here now. [*Looks around.*] Oh, where has he gone. Peter, Peter, here Peter! Oh there you are! This is Aunt Evelyn. Oh, he's only joking Aunt *Eve*lyn. He's making believe he's shy. Say some thing to Aunt *Eve*lyn, Peter."

PETER. "Hello, Aunt Evelyn."

PHYLLIS. There! [*Sits on sofa.*]

PETER. I wish your grandfather hadn't been so prolific.

[PETER *dresses upstage.* MARY *enters from stairs.*]

MARY. [*Coming Center between* PHYLLIS *and* PETER.] I waited until the last second with this—because I just want to give it to you—and let that be the end of it. [*Hands* PHYLLIS *a small box.*] Don't open it now—your grandfather gave it to me—long time ago—to wear at *my* wedding.—[*Smiles brightly.*] It's very old —but you'll love it.

[PETER *drifts Left looking at statue, puts out cigarette on table Left.*]

PHYLLIS. I know I shall, Aunt Mary. But why so soon?

MARY. Oh—I don't know—I never know where I'm liable to be when people get married.

[PHYLLIS *and* MARY *are in front of sofa.*]

PHYLLIS. Oh— [*Very sweetly.*] Thank you, Aunt Mary. I hope you don't think we came here tonight just to—

MARY. No, no.—Even if it were I wouldn't mind. And I know the next time it will be because you want to come.

PETER. Miss Herries, may I ask who did that?

MARY. [*Crossing Center.*] Which?

PETER. This one—the statue.

MARY. Troubetzkoi—Mr. Santard.

PETER. Troubetzkoi, eh? What's it supposed to be?

MARY. [*Crossing to below table Left.*] I really don't know who she is. I think it's listed in the catalogue as "Figure" or something equally enlightening.

PETER. [*Crosses to* PHYLLIS *Right Center.*] I think it's grand. Phyllis, we must get one of this fellow's things sometime.

PHYLLIS. Yes. yes—all right, darling. That's the fourth time tonight you've said that.

PETER. Is it? I must like it.

MARY. [*Crossing to chair Left Center.*] Do you like it very much, Mr. Santard?

PETER. [*With mock sadness.*] Please call me "Peter."

MARY. All right, Peter. I'll tell you what I'll do. I'll give it to you for a wedding present.

PETER. What—really?

PHYLLIS. [*Crossing to her.*] Oh, no, Aunt Mary. I won't dream of it. You simply mustn't!

MARY. [*Sits Left Center.*] No—no. It's all settled.

PHYLLIS. But you must be awfully fond of it yourself.

MARY. I am. But I want you to have it—if you like it too, Phyllis.

PHYLLIS. Oh—I like it.—[*Gives a look of disgust to* PETER.]

MARY. It's the best present I can think of for me to give you.

PHYLLIS. Honestly, Aunt Mary—after one drink of cold water, Peter wouldn't know if Troubetzkoi or Madame Toussaud did it. [*Crosses Left above table.*]

PETER. What's the difference? And anyway I know very well who did it—Troubetzkoi. [*Snaps fingers and returns to contemplating it.*]

MARY. Then that's that. [*She imitates his finger snap.*]

PETER. Have you any more Troubetzkoi's in the house?

[PHYLLIS *has crossed to in front of fireplace.*]

MARY. Oh, yes. Didn't you notice the one in the dining room?

PETER. Whereabouts?

MARY. On the sideboard.

PETER. [*Picking up brandy glass from table Left.*] I'll have another look at it.

MARY. Do.

PETER. [*As he passes into dining room, he salutes* PHYLLIS *with the glass.*] Troubetzkoi!!

PHYLLIS. [*Silent for a moment, then very formal.*] Look, Aunt Mary. We really *must* go. The Howards will be terribly offended and we can't afford that.

MARY. No, indeed!

PHYLLIS. I didn't mean it that way. Really, Aunt Mary—

MARY. That's all right.

PHYLLIS. *I* want to be friends with you—even if Mother insists on being an idiot!

MARY. [*With a laugh.*] The Howards are expecting you!

PHYLLIS. [*Looks for a moment at* MARY. *Shakes her head and goes to door up Left.*] Peter!

PETER. [*Off in dining room.*] Huh!

PHYLLIS. Say goodbye to Aunt Mary.

PETER. [*Off.*] Goodbye, Aunt Mary.

[MARY *laughs.*]

PHYLLIS. [*Up Left.*] Peter!

PETER. [*Enters from door Upper Left to in front of fireplace.*] Yes?

PHYLLIS. We're leaving!

PETER. Oh! Sorry! [*To* MARY, *crossing to Down Left close to table.*] What did you say the name of that fellow was?

MARY. Troubetzkoi.

PETER. Oh, yes.

PHYLLIS. [*Crosses to above chair Left. Quietly, shaking her head.*] Oh, you *are* a fool!

PETER. What's the matter?

PHYLLIS. [*Pointing at* MARY.] Here's someone with banks full of lovely money—and nothing to do with it except buy statues—and you go and get us a statue for a wedding present!

[*Doorbell rings.*]

PETER. [*To* MARY.] Don't you think she's a little commercial?

MARY. [*Rises.*] No, Peter.—Just frank. All our family is addicted to frankness.

PETER. Thanks for the tip. You must tell me all about the family.

PHYLLIS. Come on, Peter.

[ROSE *crosses on platform to door off Right.*]

MARY. Come and see me in a few months and pick up the Troubetzkoi.

PETER. May I come sooner than that and look at it—and look at you?

MARY. Do that! And I'll see if I need any bonds.

PETER. Did she tell you you had to buy bonds, too?

PHYLLIS. Why not? She's always buying them from *somebody*.

PETER. My God!

[MARY *laughs.* ROSE *enters from Right on platform.*]

ROSE. Madam!

MARY. [*Crosses Up Center.*] What is it, Rose?

ROSE. It's—!

HENRY. [*Enters from Right.*] I beg your pardon. I'll wait outside. [*He goes off Right.*]

MARY. [PETER *and* PHYLLIS *look at each other. A little embarrassed.*] That's a young man whom I—never mind—you're in a hurry. It's all right, Rose. Get Miss Glenning's and Mr. Santard's things. [ROSE *exits Right.* PHYLLIS *looks at* PETER *with a "What do you know."*] And now—run along, you two. Keep your "appointments." I hope I haven't made you too late.

PETER. [*Crossing Up Left to join* PHYLLIS.] Of course not. Please forget about it.

MARY. [*As she reaches entrance to hall, speaks to* HENRY.] Will you come in here?

HENRY. [*As he passes.*] I'm very sorry.

MARY. Please sit down.

[HENRY *crosses Right then Down Right—then Right Center below sofa.* MARY *goes off Right.* HENRY *sits.*]

PHYLLIS. [*Handing* PETER *box.*] Put the box in your pocket darling and be very careful.

[PHYLLIS *and* PETER *exit Right glancing back at* HENRY.]

MARY. [*Off.*] That's a lovely wrap, Phyllis.

PETER. [*Off.*] I'll remember that hopping in and out business!

[ROSE *crosses past arch to Left.*]

MARY. [*Off. Laughs.*] Please do!

PHYLLIS. [*Off.*] Good night, Aunt Mary. I'll ring you up. Honestly!

PETER. [*Off.*] Good night—and permit an old man to bless you.

MARY. [*Off—laughing.*] Good night.—[*Door slams.* MARY *enters—crosses to Down Center.*]

HENRY. [*Rises, takes cigarette case from his pocket and holds it out.*] I pawned it.—

MARY. [*Takes it.*] What a disgraceful thing to do. —And what are you going to steal next?

HENRY. My wife made some money last week.—That will see us through for a while.

MARY. Don't you ever do any work?

HENRY. I paint—but no one will touch my pictures. They're not modern enough.

MARY. You must show me some of your pictures sometime.

HENRY. I have some here. They're in the hall.—[*Goes toward arch.*] You probably didn't notice. [*He goes out Right and returns immediately from the hall with two canvases, face to face—crosses to desk.*]

[MARY *puts cigarette case on table Left.*]

MARY. [*Crosses Up Center as* HENRY *re-enters.*] —Let's see what you have. [HENRY *places one picture on desk. He holds up another picture showing a cowherd playing his pipes to a group of cows. There is a pause while she looks at them.*] Oh, those are very bad.

HENRY. [*Crossing Up Right Center.*] I know they are. You must understand that my esthetic taste is very fine. I appreciate only the best things—like your cigarette case. But I can paint nothing but these.—It's very exasperating.

MARY. It must be.

HENRY. [*Crosses to her a bit.*] Won't you buy one?

[HENRY *is Center—*MARY *is Left Center by chair.*]

MARY. You don't mean it?

HENRY. Why not?

MARY. But what should I do with it? I'd have to hide it!

HENRY. Not necessarily. Bad as they are, they have something, I think. [*Puts cow picture on floor against sofa.*]

MARY. I don't see it—whatever it is. [*Crosses below chair Left Center.*] I really don't want one.

HENRY. [*Two paces toward* MARY.] Please buy one, anyway.—

MARY. [*Retreating a pace.*] No—but of course not.—

HENRY. [*Comes closer to her.*] Yes, please.—[*She looks at him, disturbed by his peculiar insistence. At any rate there is something of the rabbit and the snake in this passing tableau.*] My wife is waiting in the street just opposite—waiting for me to call her.

MARY. [*Recovering herself.*] What on earth for?

HENRY. She wanted to thank you. And I wanted her to see some of your lovely things.

MARY. How can you let her wait out in that deathly cold?

HENRY. I didn't like to bring her without your permission. And I don't like her to see me begging.

MARY. Well, you go straight out and take her home.

HENRY. [*Not moving.*] Can't I possibly persuade you— [*Then; crosses upstage a bit.*] this one with the cows isn't so bad.

MARY. [*Shaking her head as she looks at it.*] It's peculiar enough. What is it supposed to be?

HENRY. It's a Swiss scene. In Switzerland the cowherd pipes his cows from the pasture! He plays a traditional melody. Ranz des Vaches they call it. I read about it and I thought it was a rather nice macabre idea.

MARY. You've achieved a sinister quality in it, at any rate.—How much is it?

HENRY. Five guineas. The other one is seven.

MARY. [*Laughing.*] You're really amusing. And quite absurd. They're not worth anything at all.

HENRY. They may be one day.—You never know with modern pictures.

MARY. I'm quite sure about those.

HENRY. [*Crosses to picture of cow, takes it to* MARY, *Center.*] But I must sell one tonight—whatever you think of them.—[*Holds out cow picture.*] Please buy it.—[*But he is not pleading.*]

MARY. [*After a pause.*] I'm a perfect fool.—[*She is crossing toward desk.* HENRY *puts picture behind Left Center chair then crosses to desk for check.*] What's your name? [*Writing check at desk.*]

HENRY. Henry—Abbott. The baby's Henry, too.

MARY. [*Rises, hands him check.*] Here—and please understand that I never want to see you again. Never. —You will not be admitted. It's no use speaking to me in the street. If you bother me, I shall tell the police.

HENRY. [*In spite of this he has not let go of her hand which he took when he reached for the check. He does so now, folding the check and putting it in pocket.*] Hang that in the right light and it won't be bad.— [*He crosses down a step.*]

MARY. You didn't get those shoes. Those are terrible.

HENRY. I'll be able to now.

MARY. The first thing you do is rescue that poor girl. You're a thorough brute, young man.

HENRY. She's used to it.—

MARY. More shame to you!

HENRY. You can see her from here. [*He crosses to upstage window.*] There she is.

MARY. [*Goes to downstage window.*] With the baby! Oh!! [*Gasps.*]

HENRY. Ada!!! My God!! [*He runs out Right.*]

MARY. [*Running to arch.*] Rose! Rose!

ROSE. [*Running from Left arch.*] Yes, Madam!

MARY. Run out and help him—the baby!!! [*As* ROSE *half turns to Left.*] Never mind! Take my coat! Run! [*Almost pushing her.* ROSE *runs out Right.* MARY *goes to window, thrusts shade aside. Watches.*] Oh.—[*Suddenly goes quickly out to hall again. After a second* HENRY *enters, carrying* ADA. MARY *follows to arch.*] On the sofa!

[ROSE *enters with baby, crosses to below Left Center chair.* MARY *follows to Left Center.* HENRY *carries* ADA *to sofa and places her on it. Her head is stage Right.* HENRY *is below sofa.* HENRY *has taken* ADA'S *head in his hands, shaking it, drops it, grabs her hands, almost immediately lets go, pours drink of brandy from decanter on coffee table, puts it to her lips, it dribbles back.*]

HENRY. Ada! Ada! [*Again tries unsuccessfully to give her whiskey. To* MARY.] What shall we do?

MARY. [*Quietly holding her heart—crosses to* ROSE.] Isn't there any doctor near here—somewhere, Rose?

ROSE. Yes, Madam. In the block of flats at the top of the street.

MARY. Get him! Get someone—the nurse—if there's no one there, call an ambulance.—

ROSE. Yes, Madam. [*Gives baby to* MARY. *Starts to go.*]

HENRY. [*Rises and meets* ROSE *at Center. Holding* ROSE *with one hand.*] I'll go. [*Rushes out Right.*]

ROSE. [*Looks after* HENRY—*steps toward* ADA—*turns to* MARY.] Miss Herries—

MARY. [*Almost simultaneously.*] Get that bottle of smelling salts. . . .

ROSE. Yes, Madam.

MARY. [ROSE *runs out upstairs.* MARY *tries to rub* ADA *and hold baby. She looks helplessly from* ADA *to the baby, puts baby in chair Left Center, returns to* ADA, *crosses to window—then to baby Right of chair Center. Takes baby.* ROSE *rushes in with smelling salts which she puts in front of* ADA'S *nose.* ADA *stiffens but does not come to.*] It's all my fault—all my fault for letting him—

ROSE What's the matter with her, Madam? [*Crosses to* MARY.]

MARY. Go on, go on!

[ROSE *administers smelling salts, rubs* ADA *in a very inexperienced manner.* HENRY *and* DOCTOR *enter.*]

HENRY Here! [*He does not take baby from* MARY, *but*

crosses to above sofa. DOCTOR *crosses below sofa and looks at* ADA.] Ada! Ada!

ROSE. I'll take it, Madam.

[*Crosses to* MARY. MARY *crosses Up Left Center.* MARY *gives baby to* ROSE. ROSE *goes above table Left.*]

DOCTOR. [*To* HENRY.] Exposure. [*Picks up* ADA. *Crosses Right Center.*] You'd better put her to bed at once.

MARY. Bed? She—

HENRY. You see, Doctor—

DOCTOR. [*To* ROSE.] Where's a bedroom?

MARY. [*Looks at* ROSE.] Why—

DOCTOR. Upstairs? [*This to* ROSE *with the baby. He carries* ADA *out; as he goes.*] Don't worry. Nothing serious. Needs rest and nourishment. [*To* ROSE.] Some hot soup. Chicken broth.

[DOCTOR *exits upstairs, followed by* ROSE. MARY *goes up onto platform and turns back to* HENRY *who is walking unconcernedly Down Right, lighting a cigarette.* MARY, *greatly agitated, hurries upstairs.* HENRY *calmly walks Center looking at room. Sees his painting of the cows. Picks it up. Looks about the room. Selects the mantel. Puts his picture there. Stands back looking at it. Sits Left Center chair admiring his picture. He is totally unconcerned about what has just happened.*]

CURTAIN

ACT TWO

Two weeks later—January.

The scene is the same. However, the desk is now behind the sofa at Right Center. The coffee table is to the Right of the sofa. A side chair is behind the desk and another is between the windows.

HENRY is at the desk. The doorbell rings— HENRY looks up from a paper he has been writing on—then resumes. ROSE comes from Left and crosses the room. She is dressed in street clothes. She walks, looks straight ahead, her hands folded before her.

HENRY. [*Speaking just as she reaches Center—not looking up.*] Rose. [ROSE *stops Center, facing him but not looking at him. He looks up now.*] You're all dressed up, Rose.—Why?

ROSE. I think you *know* why, Mr. Abbott.—

HENRY. Leaving us?

ROSE. I think you know I *am*, Mr. Abbott.

[*She stands there as if anxious to continue the conversation—to get something off her chest. But after a moment, he looks down at his paper.*]

HENRY. Answer the bell.

[*She hesitates for a moment, then pressing her lips, walks off Right.*]

MR. EDWARDS. [*Off stage.*] Mr. Henry Abbott here?

ROSE. [*She comes into room, and, not looking at* HENRY, *starts to cross Left toward dining room.*] People outside.

HENRY. Who are they?

ROSE. [*Not stopping.*] I don't know.

HENRY. [*Gently, as if admonishing a child.*] Rose! Ask them to come in.

[*She stops, hesitates as though she were inwardly undergoing a struggle. Then turns and goes to Left arch.*]

ROSE. [*Standing in arch, Center.*] Come in. [ROSE *exits off Left on platform.*]

[MR. EDWARDS *appears, followed by "his wife and daughter,* AGGIE." MR. EDWARDS *is a thick-set, reddish and bulbous-faced man with a hearty hoarse voice.* MRS. EDWARDS *is short, black-clad and eminently respectable looking.* AGGIE *is a thin, sharp-faced girl whose eyes and hands are rarely still.* MR. EDWARDS *is carrying a portable gramophone.*]

MR. EDWARDS. [*Crosses to Upper Left Center.*] Hello, Henry.

[HENRY *gets up.*]

MRS. EDWARDS. [*Up Center.*] How's Ada, Henry?

HENRY. Much better.

AGGIE. [*Up Right Center.*] Hello, Henry.

[HENRY *nods.*]

MRS. EDWARDS. We brought Aggie with us.

MR. EDWARDS. We thought we'd better——

MRS. EDWARDS. How's the baby, Henry?

MR. EDWARDS. Doing well, Henry?

HENRY. [*Nods.*] Ada will be glad to see you all.

MRS. EDWARDS. And we'll be awfully glad to see her—poor Ada.

MR. EDWARDS. I brought the gramophone. Thought she might like to hear some music.

MRS. EDWARDS. Layin' up in bed, you know.——

HENRY. Sit down, and I'll call Miss Herries.——

MRS. EDWARDS. Oh, Henry—the way I look.——

[*Crosses and sits Left Center chair.*]

HENRY. I shall have to ask permission to bring you upstairs.

MR. EDWARDS. Sure, Henry—that's only right!

HENRY. Sit down. [*He goes upstairs.*]

MR. EDWARDS. [*Crosses Down Center—looking over the room. AGGIE goes Left and picks up bronze on table Upper Left.*] Very nice layout. [*Crosses to Down Right puts gramophone on coffee table and hat on Left end of desk.*]

MRS. EDWARDS. I should say it is.—My—isn't it pretty!

MR. EDWARDS. [*Puts gramophone on coffee table.*] Looks like a house I stayed in once—in Melbourne in Australia.

MRS. EDWARDS. Put that down, Aggie!

MR. EDWARDS. [*Crossing to Upper Center.*] Same layout.—I'd be able to tell better if I saw the whole house. [*To* AGGIE *who is touching things on mantel.*] Aggie! I wish you would talk to her, Mother. Nice thing if somebody saw her. [*Crosses Down Right and sits in sofa.*]

MRS. EDWARDS. Father's right, Aggie. You ought to learn to behave yourself in a decent place.

[AGGIE *walks to arch Up Center. They watch her, she looks out and returns to rooms crossing to desk.*]

MR. EDWARDS. [*After another moment.*] You notice how nobody has pianos any more?

MRS. EDWARDS. [*Nodding.*] If you lived in a house with a court you'd hear the children practicing, all day long.

MR. EDWARDS. It's the wireless that's spoiled it for pianos.

MRS. EDWARDS. [*Not looking at her.*] Sit down, Aggie. Didn't you hear Henry say to sit down?

[AGGIE *crosses to Right end of sofa to fool with gramophone on coffee table.*]

MR. EDWARDS. Yep—now it's the wireless. But anything that's pushed out of a wire—sounds like it.

[AGGIE *is opening gramophone.*]

MRS. EDWARDS. Ts, ts.—Oh, leave it be!

MR. EDWARDS. [*Has risen with surprising swiftness to* AGGIE *and stands over her.*] Don't you realize there's somebody sick around here?

[AGGIE *looks frightened, stops playing with gramophone and examines other objects on coffee table. After a moment* MR. EDWARDS *starts to arch Center.*]

MRS. EDWARDS. I'll warrant we'll have to take you off your job, Aggie, and put you back in school, to learn some manners.

MR. EDWARDS. [*Looking upstairs in arch.*] That staircase—just like this house in Melbourne—in Australia. A very good sign.

MRS. EDWARDS. I never *knew* you were in Australia, Father.—

MR. EDWARDS. Sure—I must have told you. Been everywhere. [*Crosses Down Center to* MRS. EDWARDS.]

MRS.   EDWARDS.   [*Shaking   her   head,   puzzled.*] —Perhaps you did.—

MR. EDWARDS. [*Crosses Down Center level with* MRS. EDWARDS.] Didn't I ever mention about staying in this house that used to belong to Lord—Greville? Something like that.

MRS. EDWARDS. [*Thinking.*] I don't remember the name.

MR. EDWARDS. Fine feller—black sheep. [AGGIE *crosses Up Right.*] Came to Australia and made a pile of money.

MRS. EDWARDS. Never got married!

MR. EDWARDS. No—real black sheep. Lived all alone. Got peculiar in his old age with all that money. Used to keep it around the house, they said.

MRS. EDWARDS. Must have been a tough customer.

MR. EDWARDS. [*Nodding, lips pursed.*] That's what they said.—

MRS. EDWARDS. All that money around the house,— ts, ts.—

MR. EDWARDS. In gold—gold bars. [AGGIE *crosses to Center looks through arch.*] Some of 'em as long as your arm.

MRS. EDWARDS. Ts, ts.—I suppose they found it all after he died?

MR. EDWARDS. No.—I can't say they did. No.— [*Laughs.*] Stop worryin' about it, Mother! [*Crosses to Down Right below sofa.*]

MRS. EDWARDS. Well, it's interesting!—My goodness!—

MR. EDWARDS. I hope Ada ain't too sick to see us.—

[AGGIE *crosses to painting Up Left.*]

MRS. EDWARDS. Henry said she was all right—she was much better, he said.—

MR. EDWARDS. Yep—but you know Ada ain't a strong

girl. If she's been layin' in bed for two weeks—there's something wrong with her.

MRS. EDWARDS. Very nice of this lady, isn't it, Father?

MR. EDWARDS. I should say. She sounds like a real fine woman.

MRS. EDWARDS. [AGGIE *has wandered Left and is touching the things on table Left.*] Keep your hands off, Aggie!

[HENRY *comes down stairs.*]

HENRY. [*Stops Center, speaking from landing.*] Miss Herries begs to be excused. She hopes to meet you all some other time.

MRS. EDWARDS. [*Rises.*] I hope she ain't sick, Henry?

HENRY. No.—[*Gestures them to go up.*]

MR. EDWARDS. Should I bring up the gramophone, Henry?

HENRY. I don't think so—no. [*Holding place Right of Center on platform.*]

MR. EDWARDS. [*Setting it at back of sofa.*] I'll just set it here out of the way then.—

MRS. EDWARDS. [*Crosses between Left Center chair and table toward stairs.* AGGIE *drifts behind her.*] Oh—this is certainly a *beautiful* house, Henry!

MR. EDWARDS. [*Crosses below sofa—propelling* AGGIE.] Go on, Aggie.

[*Doorbell rings when* MRS. EDWARDS *is at foot of*

stairs, AGGIE *behind her on bay-window landing,* MR. EDWARDS *on hall platform.* HENRY *Right on hall platform. Bell rings second time. For some reason the four of them stop dead still. There is a pause.*]

HENRY. [*Indicates.*] Two flights up—the little room at the head of the stairs.

[*Slowly they move up again.*]

MR. EDWARDS. [*The last.*] Lots of visitors today, Henry.—

[*He is off.* HENRY *waits on the landing.* ROSE *enters and crosses. He watches her. She goes off Right. A moment later.*]

LUCY. [*Off stage.*] Hello, Rose. Is Miss Herries in?

ROSE. [*Off stage.*] Yes, Madam.

[LUCY *enters room, followed by* ROSE. *She stops on seeing* HENRY.]

HENRY. How do you do? [LUCY *nods in surprise.* LUCY *meets* HENRY *in arch.*] I'll tell Miss Herries, Rose. [*To* LUCY.] Excuse me. [*He goes upstairs.*]

LUCY. [*Crossing into room. Stopping* ROSE *as she starts off behind arch.*] Rose! Isn't that the young man Miss Herries brought in here one night?

ROSE. Yes, Madam—it is.

LUCY. [*As if she knew something now.*] Oh.—

[ROSE *goes off Left on platform.* LUCY *crosses to desk to remove her gloves.*]

MARY. [*Coming down.*] Lucy!

LUCY. [*Meets* MARY *Center below platform.*] Mary, dear.—

MARY. Not even a picture postcard! [*Kisses her.*]

LUCY. Didn't you get my letter?

MARY. No.

LUCY. [*Disturbed.*] Oh, that's too bad!

MARY. Forget about it. Have a good time?

LUCY. That letter worries me.

MARY. [*Laughs.*] Really?—You probably addressed it wrong. [*Crosses to Right end of sofa and sits.*]

LUCY. No.—Oh, well. [*Crosses to desk above couch, takes off gloves.*] How are you, Mary?

MARY. Oh, fairly well. *You* look splendid.

LUCY. Thanks. I feel as though I'd never get warm again!

MARY. Just an excuse to get back to the Riviera, isn't it?

LUCY. I'm leaving this afternoon. I'm flying to Paris. [*Crosses to Left end sofa—a bit away.*]

MARY. Oh, I'm sorry!

LUCY. That's what I wrote. I didn't think I'd have a chance to see you. Then I decided to come around for a minute anyway.

MARY. I'm glad you did!

LUCY. I just couldn't write you as I did and let it go at that. And when you didn't answer—I knew something was wrong.

MARY. What are you talking about?

LUCY. I'll tell you simply and to the point—if you'll tell me what's been going on here.

MARY. Going on?—[*After a moment she sits back.*] Please say what you have to say, Lucy, before I go completely out of my mind.—

LUCY. All right. Some days after we got to St. Moritz, a lady joined us. She had just arrived—and she had it on *excellent authority*—steady on—that you had taken a man to live with you—

MARY. [*After a moment, as though this were the last straw, murmurs.*] What?

LUCY. I laughed her down of course—told her she was a silly woman, I insulted her frightfully.—[*Slowly.*] It didn't do much good.—

MARY. But who would say a thing like that?

LUCY. She from whom all such blessings flow—your sister Emily.

MARY. Emily! It's incredible! How would she know?

LUCY. She didn't say.—

MARY. [*Very puzzled—thinking.*] Emily.—

LUCY. Women like that make mountains out of blades of grass—you know that.

MARY. Oh! Ho!

LUCY. You've traced it!

MARY. No.—My niece Phyllis—and her fiancé—were here one night. They saw him—but why would they—Oh, no!

LUCY. Saw who?

MARY. Lucy—it's true.

LUCY. What!?

MARY. I have taken a man in to live with me—and his wife and child.

LUCY. That one—you brought in here on Christmas Eve?

MARY. Hmmm. He came back with his wife. She fainted and I put her up for the night. She's been here ever since.

LUCY. [*Crosses to sofa and sits. After a pause.*] Oh, Mary, Mary. My poor Mary!

MARY. That's only part of it. My cook left me last week —and Rose gave me notice. I've been on my knees to her in the kitchen. She insists on going.

LUCY. Who are those people?

MARY. I don't know. It's become nightmarish. What will I do without Rose? I'll never replace her.—

LUCY. [*Dismissing this.*] Rose!—Throw those people out! How ill is she?

MARY. I don't know—I can't tell. I know *I've* been feeling badly the past few days. My heart has been raising red hell.—

LUCY. Oh, Mary! [*Pause, then decisively.*] It's insane! You're being used in the most ridiculous and criminal manner.

MARY. Well, goodness knows, I begged for it!

LUCY. I know you!—Throw them out! You've simply *got* to!

MARY. I suddenly feel very old and helpless. [*Doorbell.*]

LUCY. [*Quietly.*] You fool, Mary—I haven't the heart to scream at you.—

MARY. Now they've got friends upstairs—visiting. I don't know why that should bother me. But it does—intensely.

LUCY. Will you please get rid of them—and take a plane tomorrow with me? I'll wait on.

MARY. A plane?

LUCY. A train then.

[ROSE *crosses to door from Left to Right on platform.*]

MARY. I never felt more like it. I really want to.

LUCY. Fine!

MARY. Not tomorrow of course. I've got to clean up this mess. And if I go I'll close the house.

LUCY. Next week then—

MARY. Perhaps, in a week or so.

DOCTOR. [*Off stage.*] Good afternoon.

ROSE. [*Off stage.*] Good afternoon.

MARY. Now who? [*Rises, crosses to archway.*]

LUCY. You certainly have a busy house.

ROSE. [*Entering.*] It's the Doctor, Madam.

MARY. [*Right of archway.*] Oh! Go straight up, Doctor.

[ROSE *starts to lead way, getting to Center of landing.*]

DOCTOR. [*To* MARY.] Thank you. [*To* ROSE.] That's quite all right. I know the way.

[DOCTOR *goes upstairs.* ROSE *goes off Left past arch on platform.*]

LUCY. I should go—but I'm not going to—[MARY *crosses Down Center.*] until you promise to close this house and get out of here.

MARY. All right, I promise.

LUCY. Good. [*She rises and crosses Center.*] I must rush. [*Crosses to desk and gets gloves.*] I expressed everything through the St. Moritz. But there's a coat I want—and some shoes.—

MARY. Go on, then. [*Smiles wanly. Speaks simply.*] And thank you.

LUCY. Now remember—you've *promised!*

MARY. All right!

LUCY. Well—goodbye—and God bless you. [*Starts off.*] Get rid of those strange leeches.

MARY. I will.—[*As they go through the arch.*] Give my love to Phil and the children.

LUCY. Thank you, dear.—[*From now on, off stage.*] When will I hear from you?

[ROSE *enters at Right and stands Right Center.*]

MARY. I'll write.—

LUCY. The minute you've decided—I wish you could come and tell me what you think of this coat. I'm spending far too much. Goodbye—

MARY. Have a nice trip, Lucy. [*Door slams.*]

ROSE. [*As* MARY *comes in.*] Miss Herries—

MARY. [*At Center—surprised as she looks at* ROSE'S *clothes.*] Going already, Rose?

ROSE. Yes, Madam. I was just waiting to say goodbye.

MARY. [*After a moment—as if tired of the whole thing. Crosses to desk.*] Well—I suppose if you've made up your mind to leave, you'd better.

ROSE. Yes, Madam. I'm sorry. I'd like to come back in a while.

MARY. Let me have your address?

ROSE. [*Crossing Down Center.*] It's on the bill hook—in the pantry.

MARY. [*Sees* EDWARDS' *hat on desk and distastefully puts it on chair between windows.*] All right.—

ROSE. [*Crosses Down Right Center.*] Goodbye, Miss Herries.

MARY. Rose, I wish I really knew why you were leaving. Is it the work, Rose?

ROSE. I told you, Madam.

MARY. What's the matter?

ROSE. Nothing, Madam, I told you—I want to visit my sister in Newcastle.

MARY. I don't believe that. You've never *mentioned* a sister all the time you've been with me. [*Crosses in front of sofa toward* ROSE.] Now look here, Rose, I didn't intend to plead with you to stay on. But I've decided to close the house. If you'll wait a week you can go where you like and I'll be glad to take you back in about three months.

ROSE. [*With trace of eagerness.*] You're closing the house, Miss Herries?

MARY. This week.

ROSE. But excuse me, Madam— What's happening to them?

MARY. The Abbotts? They're leaving, of course.

ROSE. They are?

MARY. Oh. So it *is* the Abbotts. Why didn't you say so?

ROSE. Miss Herries—! [ROSE *cannot speak.*]

MARY. [*Crosses to* ROSE.] What is it? What are you crying for?

ROSE. Miss Herries.—I don't want to go!

MARY. Then why?

ROSE. It isn't the work, Madam, I don't mind that.—

MARY. [*Close to* ROSE.] What's wrong then? You must tell me!

ROSE. Are you sure they're leaving, Madam?

MARY. Quite sure.

ROSE. Him, too?

MARY. Yes! What *is* it, Rose? [*Taking* ROSE's *arm.* ROSE *pauses uncertainly.*] Has Mr. Abbott said anything to you?

ROSE. No, Madam.—[*Burst out.*] It ain't what he says! I can't explain what I mean, Miss Herries! There's something about him! I'm afraid.—

MARY. Afraid of what—?

ROSE. I don't know.—I'm afraid to stay here.—

MARY. What is it, Rose? Try to tell me.

ROSE. That Mrs. Abbott—

MARY. Yes.

ROSE. She's not ill, Madam. She lays up there in that bed—lookin' like she's dyin'. But she ain't ill—and never was!

MARY. Never was?

ROSE. No, Madam! There's some people always look that way—an' she's one of 'em. But I know she's not ill!

MARY. *How* do you know?

ROSE. I just do, Madam. She's been putting it on all the time!

MARY. Putting it on?

ROSE. Yes. And the baby! Did you notice something funny about it?

MARY. No.—

ROSE. Did you ever hear it cry?

MARY. [*After quite a pause, as if she just realized.*] No.—

ROSE. Neither did I! Never! I never heard it make a sound.—I think it *can't*, Miss Herries. It wants to—but it can't.

MARY. [*A quick involuntary phrase.*] Oh, no.

ROSE. Yes, Madam—that's what I think. And something else—it don't look like her. It looks foreign—like an Italian baby. But it's not hers.

MARY. How can you tell—it's just an infant?

ROSE. No, it's not. Not as young as he said! Oh, I don't know, Miss Herries! I'm just scared to death—! [*She cries again. There is a pause.*]

MARY. Rose, please stop crying.

ROSE. I'm sorry, Madam.—

MARY. I want you to pack up whatever belongs to the baby—at once.

ROSE. Yes, Madam.—

MARY. Then take a directory and see if you can find some private hospital which has an ambulance we can hire to call for Mrs. Abbott.

ROSE. [*Turns and crosses Up Center.*] Yes, Madam?

MARY. Wait a minute. [ROSE *turns.* MARY *crosses to her.*] Tell them we don't want anyone taken to the hospital. We just want to hire the ambulance and an attendant for about an hour.

ROSE. I will, Miss Herries.

MARY. Tell them we'll ring up again—and let them know—will you, Rose?

ROSE. Yes, Madam.

MARY. [*Ushers* ROSE *Up Center onto platform.*] Straight away.—Now go on and don't be afraid of anything.

ROSE. [*Turning to* MARY.] I don't want to be foolish, Madam.—As long as they're goin'.—

MARY. It's all right. I'm sorry you didn't tell me all this before.

ROSE. I didn't want to interfere, Miss Herries. I thought perhaps you had some special reason.

MARY. I've just been very stupid, Rose.—Now please go and do as I asked.

ROSE. Yes, Madam,

[*Turns and goes off Left.* MARY *watches her off—then suddenly goes to stairs, reaches landing and is about to go up when she pauses as the sound of voices reaches her. She hesitates for a moment then returns to room, standing by fireplace. Lights dim from here to end of Act II.*]

MRS. EDWARDS. [*Off.*] Goodbye. Aggie, say goodbye to Ada.

AGGIE. [*Off.*] Goodbye, Ada.

MR. EDWARDS. [*Off.*] That's a good girl.

MRS. EDWARDS. [*Off.*] Mind your manners and you'll keep your friends. Ha! Ha!

MR. EDWARDS. [*Off.*] Goodbye, Ada. [*Door slams off Left. Pause.*]

MRS. EDWARDS. [*Off stage.*] We shouldn't have come, Father.—

MR. EDWARDS. [*Off stage.*] She's a pretty sick girl.

MRS. EDWARDS. [*Off stage.*] Ts, ts.—I hope we haven't done any harm.

MR. EDWARDS. [*Off.*] Country air—that's what she needs.

MRS. EDWARDS. [*Off.*] Leave that alone, Aggie!

MR. EDWARDS. [*Off.*] There ain't an ounce of flesh on her. [*As he finishes he comes into view, crosses to Upper Left Center.*]

MRS. EDWARDS. You'd hardly know what was whiter— her or the sheets. I—

[*She, too, has come into view and stops Up Center seeing* MARY. *Behind* MRS. EDWARDS *is* AGGIE; *from dining room comes* HENRY, *crossing to above Left table.*]

HENRY. Miss Herries, these are Ada's friends; Mr. and Mrs. Edwards and their daughter, Aggie.

[MARY *nods.*]

MR. EDWARDS. How do you do, Ma'am?

MRS. EDWARDS. We've just been up to *see* Ada. My— she's a sight, isn't she?

HENRY. [*Crosses to Center to* MRS. EDWARDS.] I'm afraid the excitement was too much.

[AGGIE *drifts to above desk.*]

MRS. EDWARDS. I hope we haven't done any harm.—

MR. EDWARDS. [*Crosses to above table Left.*] She's just all in! Not an ounce of flesh on her, Ma'am.

HENRY. [*Paces Down Left Center.*] It occurred to me up stairs. We're looking for a cook. If I may take the liberty of recommending Mrs. Edwards—

MRS. EDWARDS. Now, Henry.

HENRY. I know she's worked in the very best homes.

MRS. EDWARDS. [*Crosses Down Right Center.*] As a cook only, Ma'am.

HENRY. And with Aggie to help—if Rose insists on going—I thought we could struggle along for a while.

MARY. Thank you. I won't need anyone. I'm closing the house.

HENRY. [*Paces toward* MARY, *below Left Center chair*.] Really, Miss Herries?

MARY. [*Below Left chair*.] I'm not well, either. I need a rest.

HENRY. That's too bad.

MARY. I'm glad your friends are here. They can help move Ada. I'm hiring a private ambulance.

HENRY. You mean move her today?

MARY. Oh, yes!

HENRY. Where shall I take her?

MARY. Take her home!

HENRY. I would—willingly—but, we have no home. [MARY *starts to speak*.] We were so far behind on the rent—we were dispossessed a week ago, I thought I told you.—

MARY. I'm afraid your troubles can't concern me any longer. Take Ada any place you please.

MRS. EDWARDS. That's a pretty hard way to talk, Miss Herries.

MARY. You must understand, I don't want to seem brutal—but I think Mrs. Abbott is well enough to go now—and I wish you all good day.

MRS. EDWARDS. I'm sure you've been kindness itself, Miss Herries. Ada knows that, I'm sure. But to move her now would be to kill her, that's all. Any movement and she'll drop at your feet.

HENRY. Besides we have no place to go—as I've told you.

MARY. [*Controlling herself.*] But this lady—

MRS. EDWARDS. Oh, Lord, Miss Herries—we only have two rooms—

MR. EDWARDS. That's a good idea, Ma'am! There ain't space now to swing a cat in!

AGGIE. [*Goes Right above desk.*] Popper coughs all night, anyway.

MRS. EDWARDS. Keep still, Aggie.

MR. EDWARDS. And then there's the kid, mind you!

MARY. [*To* HENRY.] I don't care to discuss it! You will get Ada out of here today!

[HENRY *looks at her steadily.*]

MRS. EDWARDS. It might be life and death you know. Do you think she ought—?

MARY. I told you I didn't care to discuss it! [MR. ED-WARDS *crosses to fireplace.* MARY *crosses to* HENRY *on line. To* HENRY.] I believed your bad luck stories—and I've done everything in my power to help you! I think it's pretty obvious that you've imposed on me in the crudest way!

HENRY. I'm sorry you think that.

MARY. You will please oblige me by getting out of here as quickly as possible.

HENRY. That's more easily said than done.—

MARY. Why you—! Leave at once, all of you!

[*They do not move.* MRS. EDWARDS *looks about her.*]

MRS. EDWARDS. [*After pause. Crosses to desk—* AGGIE *drifts a pace Right.*] Such a fine big house, Ma'am. It's wonderful how clean it is with only one help.

MR. EDWARDS. [*Crosses to* MARY *one step.*] Yep. I was telling Mother—that's my wife, Mrs. Edwards over here, how much it looks like a house I stayed in once in Melbourne, in Australia.

MARY. [*To* HENRY.] Will you please—!

MR. EDWARDS. [HENRY *crosses Up Left of arch.* EDWARDS *makes small movement toward* MARY.] It's the staircase made me think of it—same layout. Used to be a private house. Turned into a lodging house later —when I stayed there.

MARY. [*To* EDWARDS.] Leave immediately, or I shall call the police!

MR. EDWARDS. Lady who ran it—she was a left-over from the old day. A real character, Ma'am. I stayed on the top floor [MARY *crosses Up Left Center to ring bell.* MR. EDWARDS *follows to Upper Left.*]—that was the cheapest in those times.—

[MARY *goes to the bell. Just before she reaches it,* HENRY *puts his hand out gently and covers it. They have somehow formed a semi-circle about her.*]

MARY. [*To* HENRY.] How dare you!

[DOCTOR *comes down stairs and stands at Upper Center below platform with the rest.* MARY *sees him and reacts.*]

MRS. EDWARDS. [*As* MARY *reacts to* DOCTOR'S *entrance.*] Would you believe it, Miss Herries—he's never told me a word of this!

MR. EDWARDS. Well, the old lady used to start from the bottom floor in the morning. [MARY *turns to see* MR. EDWARDS *coming toward her.*] Knock, knock, knock—how do you like your ham and eggs this morning, sir? Thank you, sir. [MARY *starts backing Down Center.*] Second floor. Knock, knock, knock. How do you like your ham and eggs this morning, sir. [*As* MARY *has backed Down Center,* HENRY, MRS. EDWARDS *and* DOCTOR *have joined* MR. EDWARDS *in their slow walk forcing* MARY *down stage. They have her surrounded.* AGGIE *is Down Right.*] Thank you, sir. Third floor.—

MARY. [*With back to audience. To* HENRY *who is Upper Center.*] This is monstrous. What do you want of me?

MR. EDWARDS. [*Down Left.*] Well Ma'am, by the time she reached me—I was mighty glad to get myself a cup of tea! [*Laughs.*]

MRS. EDWARDS. [*Right Center.*] He was a one when I married him, Miss Herries!

MARY. What do you want?

HENRY. [*Comes to Center.*] What about my pay for all these weeks?

MARY. Pay—?

HENRY. My pay.

MRS. EDWARDS. His pay.—

MR. EDWARDS. [Sings.]
    "When the time comes to pay—
        You must pay.—"

[MARY staggers slightly. She looks around at them.]

MARY. [Starts to speak, but doesn't. She puts her hand to her heart—then looks around at the others. They are all watching her, quietly, starts to speak again—then bends over slightly as if in pain. Stands gasping.] Oh! [Then groans and staggers to couch, moves toward desk with arm outstretched but suddenly sinks to couch —half lying.] Oh, please! In the drawer—-the green bottle –! [Tries to point to the desk drawer.] Oh, quickly, please! [She is choking. Suddenly with a deep groan she collapses in the couch with head toward Center stage. They look at her.]

MRS. EDWARDS. Ts, ts, ts—poor woman.—

MR. EDWARDS. Luck—-! The minute I laid eyes on that staircase I knew it!

[HENRY snaps fingers to DOCTOR, who bends and touches her heart, who straightens and:]

DOCTOR. Still going. [Crosses to Left end desk.]

HENRY. Take her upstairs. [He gives EDWARDS the key.]

MR. EDWARDS. Sure, Henry—you bet.

[*Bends to pick her up.* DOCTOR *helps.* AGGIE *who has been standing over her—now kneels and claws at* MARY'S *bracelet.*]

AGGIE. Gimme that!

MR. EDWARDS. [*Pushes her away.*] Why don't you behave yourself?

MRS. EDWARDS. You're just like a little *animal,* Aggie!

MR. EDWARDS. [*Takes bracelet, looks at it, starts to pocket it.*] It's a cheap one.

HENRY. [*Who has walked to Center.*] Let me see.— [*Looks and throws it to* AGGIE, *who is Down Right.*] There now be quiet.

MR. EDWARDS. [*Pulls* MARY *to sitting position,* DOCTOR *takes her under arm.* EDWARDS *by feet.*] Upsa-daisy!

MRS. EDWARDS. Don't hurt yourself, Father.

MR. EDWARDS. [*As he goes up to landing carrying* MARY.] Oh, you're not such a heavy old lady.—Say, goodbye to everybody. [*As he goes up sings under his breath.*]
"Where are the friends that—that we used to know
 Long long ago—long long ago.—
 Where are—"

HENRY. [*Crosses to bell Left of arch.*] Sh, sh, sh, sh, sh.—

[DOCTOR *and* MR. EDWARDS *go up carrying* MARY.]

MRS. EDWARDS. [*Crosses, sits sofa.*] Came awful sudden, didn't it, Henry? Very unexpected. Saved a *lot* of trouble I should say.—

HENRY. [*Rings bell. To* AGGIE *who is examining necklace.*] Put that away, please!

MRS. EDWARDS. [*Settling herself on the couch properly.*] Sit down, Aggie.

[AGGIE *sits desk chair.* HENRY *takes bills from pocket and counts some off. Crosses to center. Holds bills in his hand.* ROSE *enters from up Left door stops level with* HENRY *and looks around.*]

HENRY. Miss Herries asked me to give you this, Rose. Unless you changed your mind and stayed.—

ROSE. Why—Miss Herries wanted me to stay on a week—she asked me to.—

HENRY. I know—we thought of taking Mrs. Abbott home today—but that's impossible. [*Watches her face.*] I know you complained about us, Rose. Miss Herries told me, I convinced her that you were wrong. Well, which is it? Will you stay? If not—this lady is ready to take your place.

ROSE. [*After a pause.*] I'll go.—

HENRY. [*Hands her money.*] Here, then.

ROSE. I've *been* paid.

HENRY. I persuaded Miss Herries to give you this—in place of the extra week. [ROSE *takes the money.*] I'm not as bad as you think, Rose. But as long as you can't bear the sight of us—you'd *better* go. [ROSE *turns un-*

certainly and starts Left.] Did you order the ambulance?

ROSE. [*Stopping.*] No.

HENRY. Whom did you call?

ROSE. St. Mary's Hospital—

HENRY. As long as you've spoken to them—would you call again before you leave and ask them not to come on— Never mind, I'll call them myself.—St. Mary's Hospital.—Thank you, Rose.

[ROSE *does not leave immediately.*]

HENRY. Goodbye.

[HENRY *watches* ROSE *off.* AGGIE *follows her to arch, stands looking after her.*]

MRS. EDWARDS. Very nicely done, Henry.—Come away from there, Aggie!

[AGGIE *crosses to window.* DOCTOR *comes in from stairs. Stops Up Center.*]

HENRY. [*Taking money out—to* DOCTOR.] The maid, Rose. [*To* MRS. EDWARDS.] Call St. Mary's Hospital. Paddington.

MRS. EDWARDS. Yes, Henry. [*Crosses to desk as she speaks next line to* DOCTOR.] The maid will be coming out of the basement.

HENRY. [*Gives* DOCTOR *money.*] Here.

DOCTOR. 'k you.

HENRY. Don't lose her.

[DOCTOR *goes off Right.*]

MRS. EDWARDS. [*Looking in phone book.*] Aggie, come
away from that window.

HENRY. Sit down!

[AGGIE *sits chair scared.* HENRY *crosses to fireplace.
Downstairs comes a strange white figure. It is* ADA *in a
nightgown. She comes into the room, doing almost a
little dance, at Center. A sharp laugh from* ADA *draws*
MRS. EDWARDS' *attention to her.*]

MRS. EDWARDS. [*At phone.*] Ada—you're going to
catch your death of cold walking around here barefoot!
Paddington 7831, please.—Thank you. [ADA *really begins to dance, around center of room. She takes a little
springing side step around the room, holding the sides
of her nightgown.*] Now that's enough, Ada—the floor
is awfully draughty! [ADA *suddenly begins to laugh—
a strange animalic laugh.*] Ada!

[ADA *dances toward* HENRY, *who has crossed to Down
Left Center.*]

HENRY. Keep still!!

[HENRY *almost simultaneously has hit her across the
mouth with the back of his hand. She gives a low cry,
clasping both her hands to her mouth, and almost
doubled up,* ADA *crosses to console Up Left, whim-
pering. She looks very much like an animal looking for
a place to hide.* HENRY *has gone to* MRS. EDWARDS.
Down the stairs comes MR. EDWARDS *heralding his ap-
proach by whistling* "Long, long ago." HENRY *crosses
up foot of stairs, takes key from* EDWARDS.]

MR. EDWARDS. [*Crosses to window above desk and looks out.*] Oh, that's fine.—There goes Rose and there goes Doc. [*He leaves the window and crosses to gramophone. Picks it up and crosses above desk to table Left —where he places it on table, cranks it.*]

HENRY. What's the matter, don't they answer? [*Crosses to* MRS. EDWARDS.]

MRS. EDWARDS. Ringing.—Hello? St. Mary's Hospital? This is the maid who called you a little while ago about an ambulance for an invalid. Montague Square? Yes.

HENRY. Never mind, they took her in a taxi.

MRS. EDWARDS. Well please never mind—they took her in a taxi—

HENRY. To her own Doctor.

[EDWARDS *puts gramophone on table. Takes crank out of pocket and winds.*]

MRS. EDWARDS. To her own Doctor.

HENRY. Make sure the ambulance hasn't left.

MRS. EDWARDS. The ambulance hasn't left has it? Thank you. [*Hangs up. To* HENRY.] No. They take their time.

MR. EDWARDS. [*Having placed the gramophone on table winds it.*] What's the matter, Ada?

HENRY. [*Going to* ADA, *who meets him Up Left Center.*] Never mind. [*Puts his arm around her. She responds but he quickly turns to business. To* MRS. ED-

WARDS.] Get the baby out of here. [*He crosses to window.*]

[ADA *crosses Left.*]

MR. EDWARDS. [*Unlocking clasps on gramophone.*] That's the trouble, Henry. Can't you just forget about it?

MRS. EDWARDS. [*Rises and crosses Up Center.*] No, Henry's right, Father. It's just a nuisance here, poor little thing.

MR. EDWARDS. What about Ada, Henry?

HENRY. Ada stays.

MRS. EDWARDS. What for, Henry? She's done her job.

MR. EDWARDS. Henry's right, Mother. You wouldn't want Ada roaming around the streets.

[MRS. EDWARDS *exits upstairs.*]

HENRY. [*Crosses to* MR. EDWARDS.] See that the Italian woman gets the baby back tonight.

MR. EDWARDS. Whatever you say, Henry.

HENRY. Shutters nailed in her room?

MR. EDWARDS. Coming up, Henry. [*Lifting lid of gramophone as if it were covering a big surprise. And that's the way he talks.*] There you are, Henry!— Ain't that nice?

[*Without replying* HENRY *takes a hammer and some nails out of record compartment in gramophone.*]

MR. EDWARDS. [*Taking a record from cover slot, puts*

it on the disc. Calls up the stairs.] I'm going to board over the window tomorrow anyway, Henry—! [*Returns to gramophone, starts it going. It is an orchestra playing*—MR. EDWARDS *leans over, listening*—ADA *listens.*] I'm crazy about that record— Ain't it nice, Ada? [ADA *who has been listening and moving her head to the rhythm now starts to dance again.* MRS. EDWARDS *is heard coming down the stairs.*]

MRS. EDWARDS. Oh, he's a sweet little feller— Oh, he's a sweet little feller. [AGGIE *meets* MRS. EDWARDS *at Center trying to see baby.*] Go away, Aggie! Frightening the poor little chap. [MRS. EDWARDS *goes to sofa, sits, talking to baby.*]

MR. EDWARDS. [*Whistling he goes to* MRS. EDWARDS.] Cootchie—cootchie—coo. [*Tickles baby.*]

MRS. EDWARDS. [*Slapping* MR. EDWARDS' *hand.*] Now, now, now! [AGGIE *is at up Left listening to music.* ADA *has come Center, swaying to the music.* MR. EDWARDS *goes to* ADA. MRS. EDWARDS *continues her baby talk throughout.*] Oh, isn't he a sweet little baby. Whoooo. —*Sweet* little feller. Whoooo—et cetera, et cetera. [ADA *and* MR. EDWARDS *start dancing*—ADA *breaks out into an exultant laugh.*]

CURTAIN

ACT THREE

Scene: The same room— The arrangement of the furniture is the same as in the Prologue. The only exception is that there are no "moderns" on the back right wall. There is a solitary "old master" there.

It is an afternoon during the following summer.

MRS. EDWARDS *is seated in chair Left of desk, peeling potatoes.*

MR. EDWARDS *is seated Left reading a newspaper.*

MARY HERRIES *sits in Left Center. She is in a half-daze, an unbelieving dream. The other two pay no attention to her as long as she keeps quiet. Finally, she attempts, slowly, to rise.* EDWARDS *notices this, pays no attention, lets her struggle and rise.* MRS. EDWARDS *rises.* MARY *looks at* MRS. EDWARDS *and sits. Then* MR. EDWARDS *resumes his reading.*

The doorbell rings, followed by two knocks on the door knocker. A trace of a glance passes between the EDWARDS, *a ray of hope is visible in* MARY. MRS. EDWARDS *goes to the window and then goes to the door. There is a pause, then she returns with the mail.* MRS.

*EDWARDS has risen and crossed to Upper
Center to meet* MRS. EDWARDS.

MARY'S *eyes follow the letters as they pass
from* MRS. EDWARDS *to* MR. EDWARDS *and
then back to the desk, in a neat pile.* MR. ED-
WARDS *returns to his newspaper at chair Left.
She looks for a time at the letters on the desk
and finally at* EDWARDS *who nods a solemn
"No, no."* MRS. EDWARDS *takes her potatoes
out Left. That closes the incident and there is
inaction until the door is heard to open.* MRS.
EDWARDS *goes to door and meets* HENRY, *who
enters.* HENRY *pays no attention to* MARY, *but
questions* MRS. EDWARDS. *What they say is as
much for* MARY'S *benefit as for anyone else's.*
HENRY *carries a portfolio. They both stand
Center on platform.*

HENRY. Is Miss Herries in?

MRS. EDWARDS. [*A pause, during which* MR. EDWARDS
slowly rises and looks at MARY.] Oh, no, sir—Miss
Herries is traveling.

HENRY. Is that so? I had no idea.

MRS. EDWARDS. [ADA *enters slowly and sits in front of
fireplace.*] Yes, sir. She left for America three weeks
ago. From there she was going to South America—and
from there to Australia.

HENRY. [*Looking about the room.*] Really! Strange
she didn't let us know.

MRS. EDWARDS. [*Very quietly and for* MARY'S *ears.*]

Miss Herries had a bad nervous breakdown, sir. She wouldn't see anyone. She left very suddenly.

HENRY. Well! I'm sorry to hear it.

MRS. EDWARDS. Yes, sir. We're closing the house for the time being.

HENRY. You are the—?

MRS. EDWARDS. Housekeeper, sir.

HENRY. Thank you. Very good! [*Crosses to desk puts portfolio on desk, looks at mail, never looking at* MARY. MRS. EDWARDS *crosses to Upper Right Center.* MR. EDWARDS *crosses to above table Left.* MARY *looks at* HENRY *in the manner of a paralytic almost—an unwavering, dull stare, her head moving very slightly from side to side.* HENRY *crosses and addresses* MARY *as if she had just appeared, very much as if he were dealing with a child.*] Well! How do you feel, Miss Herries? [*She gives no sign she has heard.*] How do you feel?

MARY. [*After a long time, very low.*] Let me go!—

HENRY. Let you go where, Miss Herries?

MARY. [*After another long time.*] What do you want?

HENRY. We want you to get well as soon as possible, Miss Herries. You know that. [*A slight pause, after which he looks up at* MRS. EDWARDS.] I'm afraid she's not much better, Mrs. Edwards.

MRS. EDWARDS. [*Crosses Down Right Center.*] No, sir, I'm afraid not.

HENRY. [*To* MARY.] The nurse tells me you haven't been eating well. [MARY *slowly looks at* MRS. EDWARDS, *then back to* HENRY.] You should, you know.—It's very important.

MARY. What do you want?

MRS. EDWARDS. I do think she seems to be more herself, sir.

HENRY. [*Nods.*] Do you understand what we are saying, Miss Herries?

[*After a pause,* MARY *slowly nods grimly. There is an immediate reaction on all of them.*]

MR. EDWARDS. Well, that's fine!

MRS. EDWARDS. I knew it!—

HENRY. I'm so glad. You're pulling through at last, Miss Herries.—You'll be up and about in no time now.

MARY. Let me go!—Let me go!! Let me go!!!

[HENRY *looks at* MRS. EDWARDS *and shakes his head.*]

HENRY. [*Takes pen and paper from pocket.*] Will you sign this paper, Miss Herries? [*She looks at them, uncomprehendingly.* MR. EDWARDS *crosses between Left Center chair and table with his newspaper. He places newspaper on* MARY'S *lap and stands at her Left.*] Will you sign it now so your affairs can be taken care of? Here, please.—[*Points out place.*]

MRS. EDWARDS. [*Crosses to* MARY, *takes pen from* HENRY, *who has moved Right.*] I'll help. dear.—[*Puts pen in her hand, and holds the back of her fist.*] Go on.—

[MARY *remains motionless, only her heavy breathing can be heard.*]

HENRY. Sign, Miss Herries. It's best.

MARY. Will you let me—go.—I won't tell.—

HENRY. Go on, Miss Herries.—

MRS. EDWARDS. Here we go.—"Mary," a nice "M" now.

MARY. No.—No.—

HENRY. You must, Miss Herries—do you hear?

MRS. EDWARDS. "Mary"— [*Trying to guide pen.*]

MARY. No.—No.—[*Suddenly she gets up—screaming, spilling pen, paper and newspaper on floor.*] No—! [MRS. EDWARDS *grabs* MARY'S *shoulders and forces her to sit again.*]

MRS. EDWARDS. Stop it, you old—

[HENRY *almost hits* MRS. EDWARDS *for being so rough with* MARY. MRS. EDWARDS *goes above* MARY'S *chair.*]

MR. EDWARDS. Here we are now.—[*Picking up pen, paper, newspaper from floor. He places them on* MARY'S *lap. Puts pen in her hand. Prompts.*] "Mary"—

MARY. [*With every bit of resolution and finality but still in a dull, weak voice.*] No. No.

[*There is a pause. All look at* HENRY *except* MARY.]

HENRY. [*Quietly.*] Tomorrow, then. Or the day after. [*He takes pen, paper and newspaper from* MARY. *To the others.*] Take her out. [*He goes to desk, puts pen and paper there.*]

MRS. EDWARDS. Don't be afraid, Miss Herries, I'll take care of you. I'm here.

[*They help her to rise and help her toward the stairs.*]

MR. EDWARDS. That's a good girl.

[*They are crossing Up Center.*]

MRS. EDWARDS. We'll have a nice little walk.

[MRS. EDWARDS *and* MARY *go upstairs.* MR. EDWARDS *stops on landing.* HENRY *returns to papers at desk.* ADA *lingers, crossing to Center.* HENRY *looks up and talks to her in somewhat the same way he has talked to* MARY.]

HENRY. Hello, Ada. Everything all right?

ADA. Yes, Henry!

HENRY. You like it here?

ADA. Yes, Henry!

HENRY. So do I. [*Pause.*] Ada.

ADA. Yes, Henry?

HENRY [*Crossing to* ADA *Up Center. As if he were suggesting a game.*] Go upstairs and watch—and listen!

ADA. Yes, Henry! [*She goes, eager to do what he asks.*]

[HENRY *crosses to Upper Left gets picture and places it in front of fireplace—then crosses to desk and sits.* EDWARDS *looks back up the stairs—turns to* HENRY— *shakes his head.*]

HENRY. Don't be impatient, Edwards.

MR. EDWARDS. [*Crossing down to Left of desk.*] Whatever you say, Henry.

HENRY. Miss Herries is a very fine woman. She has character. She has *strength*—

MR. EDWARDS. That's true—but—

[HENRY *is reading the mail.*]

HENRY. Imagination—hope. She still has hope, Edwards.

MR. EDWARDS. Stubborn.

HENRY. *Time,* Edwards.

MR. EDWARDS. Perhaps.

HENRY. There is a dealer from Paris coming this afternoon to look at the Whistler. [*Gestures to the picture propped against the fireplace.*]

MR. EDWARDS. Here?

HENRY. He will also see Miss Herries—talk to her.

MR. EDWARDS. *Talk* to her, Henry!

HENRY. It would be comforting to have Miss Herries realize that if she ever should be in a position to appeal to anyone—no one would believe her.

MR. EDWARDS. Don't like it.

HENRY. Well, I'm going to try it, Edwards. [*Looks through letter.*] Ah! Lucy Weston is returning to London. [*This announcement worries* EDWARDS, *who crosses away a bit and turns back to* HENRY.] Dear Lucy. I shall look forward to seeing her again. [*He notices* EDWARDS' *worry.*] What is it, Edwards?

EDWARDS. It's about leaving this place.

HENRY. *You* may, if you want to.

EDWARDS. I didn't mean that. [*Pause. Pulls chair Left of desk up a bit and sits.*] How was Paris?

HENRY. Very nice.

EDWARDS. Buy any pictures?

HENRY. Sold a few.

EDWARDS. Mind if I see the list?

HENRY. All right. [*Gives list to* EDWARDS.]

MR. EDWARDS. [*He is impressed by list.*] Quite right, Henry. There's a time to. After awhile the odds keep stretching.

HENRY. [*Quietly and patiently.*] We *live* here, Edwards. We are Miss Herries' best friends—her only friends—in London. The only ones who have cared for her since her—illness. I should think that idea would appeal to *you*. *Steady* employment. [*Doorbell.*] That should be the man from Bernstein et Fils.

MR. EDWARDS. [*Crossing up into bay window and calling upstairs.*] Mother!

HENRY. [*Who has crossed to the window.*] Wait! It isn't. It's Peter.

MR. EDWARDS. Peter!

[MRS. EDWARDS *comes down the stairs.*]

HENRY. [*Picks up portfolio and papers.*] Show him in. [HENRY *exits to dining room Left.* MR. EDWARDS *goes upstairs.* MRS. EDWARDS *waits until* MR. EDWARDS *is on the way then goes to the hall. All this is done casually.*]

MRS. EDWARDS. [*Off.*] Yes, sir?

PETER. [*Off.*] I'm Mr. Santard.

MRS. EDWARDS. [*Off.*] Oh, yes, sir. You rang up several weeks ago.

PETER. [*Off.*] That's right.

MRS. EDWARDS. [*Off.*] Will you come in, sir?

PETER. [*Off.*] Thank you. [*He enters to Center of platform.* MRS. EDWARDS *follows.*] You are the—

MRS. EDWARDS. The housekeeper, sir. Mrs. Edwards.

PETER. I told *Mrs.* Santard, Miss Herries' niece, what you said and we all thought it would be a good idea for one of us to hop around sometime and get the details.

MRS. EDWARDS. Yes, sir.

PETER. America, you said?

MRS. EDWARDS. Yes, sir. I believe she had a friend there —in California.

PETER. You don't know who—or where? We're going to America ourselves—

MRS. EDWARDS. She didn't say.—

PETER. She left no forwarding address of any kind?

MRS. EDWARDS. Only Thomas Cook in Melbourne, sir—in April.

PETER. Australia?

MRS. EDWARDS. Yes, sir. She's going around the world.

PETER. And nothing until then?

MRS. EDWARDS. Not that I know, sir.—I mean not with me.

PETER. [*Crosses to table Left.*] Do you know why Miss Herries left so suddenly?

MRS. EDWARDS. [*Counters to Center.*] No, sir. Her heart was bothering her I think—and the maid told me she was awful nervous.

PETER. Do you know where that maid is?

MRS. EDWARDS. With Miss Herries I believe, sir.

PETER. Was Miss Herries being treated by a doctor?

MRS. EDWARDS. Not that I know, sir. I came just before she left—and all I was told was to close the house and wait till Mr. Henry Abbott dismissed me.

PETER. Mr. Henry Abbott? Who's that?

MRS. EDWARDS. He's the agent, sir, in charge of the pictures.

PETER. What do you mean—in charge of them?

MRS. EDWARDS. I believe he's selling them, sir.

PETER. [*After a pause*] Is he here now?

MRS. EDWARDS. Yes, sir. Would you like to see him?

PETER. Please.

[*She goes out Left.* PETER *takes a cigarette from a case in his pocket, lights it and crosses Right.* HENRY *comes in from up Left stops Center.*]

HENRY. Mr. Santard?

PETER. How do you do? I believe I saw you here one night—some time ago.

HENRY. Oh, yes. I brought some of my pictures to show Miss Herries—

PETER. Can you throw light on her mysterious disappearance?

HENRY. [*Laughs.*] I think so.—Please sit down. [*Indicates Left Center chair.*]

PETER. Thank you. [*Sits chair Left Center.*]

HENRY. I'm sorry I wasn't here when you rang up this morning.

PETER. You see, my wife sent her aunt an invitation to our wedding and received a letter from the house-keeper!

HENRY. [*Crosses to desk. Makes notations on paper on desk.*] I'm awfully sorry. I must have been away—on the Continent. Had I been here when your invitation came, I—

PETER. That's all right. What's the old lady up to— sneaking away like that?

HENRY. She did, didn't she? [*Laughs.*] But I can't say I blame her.

PETER. What happened?

HENRY. Well—nothing particularly. She had been fed up for a long time, I think, and she had been planning this trip.

PETER. I understand you are selling her pictures?

HENRY. Just a few—I am also buying others. But I want you to believe that financially I have no interest in the matter.

PETER. Of course.

HENRY. I mean, I am doing this for nothing.

PETER. [*Slight pause.*] Do you know why she didn't come to the wedding?

HENRY. Yes.—[*Smiles.*] It isn't difficult. I feel greatly responsible, to an extent. [*Pause. Crosses in front of desk and sits on it.*] I'm afraid we'll have to turn psychological for a beginning.—

PETER. Whatever you say.

HENRY. Well then—you know something about Miss Herries—

PETER. I met her only once. I liked her immensely.

HENRY. A very fine, gentle, sweet woman.

PETER. That's what I thought—

HENRY. But a lonely woman. I seem to be delivering a lecture on—

PETER. No—go ahead.

HENRY. An old maid, afraid of being a polite nuisance to her friends. A sensitive middle-aged woman— No relative but a sister— Emily—

PETER. [*Nods.*] My mother-in-law.

HENRY. Whom she hasn't seen for years.

PETER. I wish I could say the same. I can understand that.

HENRY. Well, Miss Herries had a great fondness for my wife—

PETER. Oh—

HENRY. [*Crosses to Center.*] I should explain my position here—Miss Herries is a very generous woman. You probably know that she befriended both my wife and myself—

PETER. No, I didn't.

HENRY. She lent us money—enabled me to make a few commissions—and when my wife was ill kept her here. [PETER *nods.*] I stayed too, of course, and here's where I come in, and why I say I feel great responsibility.

PETER. [*Leans forward.*] I think I understand!

HENRY. [*Sparring.*] Really?

PETER. Please go on.

HENRY. In some way I was seen here, casually by someone, who immediately spread the most damnable silly rumor, that Miss Herries had taken a man to live with her.

PETER. I know. That was Phyllis—my then fiancée. My now wife.

HENRY. I'm sorry.

PETER. You're right. *She's* damned sorry about it now. Her mother knew she had been here and kept pumping her until Phyllis happened to mention it—just gossip, I thought.

HENRY. I'm afraid so.—One of Miss Herries' friends told her and that hurt her so, I believe, that it was the real reason for her "mysterious disappearance," as you say.

PETER. Yes, yes, I see.

HENRY. [*Crosses to desk—gets list.*] So—she went, leaving me certain items in her collection to dispose of. I'm to deposit the money in Blakely's Bank and send a report to Australia in April. It's quite a responsibility.

PETER. Sounds like it.

HENRY. [*Crosses to Center—*PETER *rises and crosses to meet him.*] Here's her list. You can see she's stipulated the minimum amounts to be obtained on each—and quite a few of these prices are pre-war.

PETER. I wouldn't know a thing about it—except that she has some pretty fine stuff.

HENRY. [*Nods.*] Most of it is extremely desirable. But art collectors don't pay as much as they used to.

PETER. I guess you art collectors were the first to feel the pinch of hard times.

HENRY. Both as artist and agent I can tell you, Mr. Santard. You're most emphatically right.

[*They both laugh.*]

PETER. Great stuff, anyway. [*Giving list back to* HENRY —*crosses Left.*] I had a fine time here, picking out things I'd like to own.

HENRY. I know! If ever temptation worried me, it did in this house. [*Puts list back on desk.*]

PETER. [*Pointing to Upper Left wall.*] There was a swell looking painting on that wall— [*Crossing Up Left between Left Center chair and table.*]

HENRY. An El Greco. That unfortunately was sold to a museum in Brussels.

PETER. Oh, yes. And a Ming horse.

HENRY. Alas, that too is gone.

PETER. [*Crosses Center.*] There were a few other things that hit me. I remember those two particularly.

HENRY. [*Smiling.*] Well— [*Getting list from desk.*] There are a few things, if you feel inclined—

PETER. Not a chance—but let's see anyway. [*Takes list from* HENRY, *looks at it and whistles.*] Whew— I'm just a poor bond salesman—

HENRY. [*Laughs*]. I think Miss Herries might consider a reduction—for a relative.

PETER. [*Laughs.*] Yes, I suppose she might. Oh, say— there's one thing I could be interested in. There was a statue on this table. I forget who did it. [*Points to table Left.*]

HENRY. [*Dressing Left a bit.*] A statue?

PETER. I remember—Troubetzkoi!

HENRY. Oh, yes.—

PETER. Does that happen to be in stock?

HENRY. Oh, yes. There it is. [*Points Up Right.*]

PETER. [*Crosses to Upper Right.* HENRY *counters Up Center.*] Oh, there. Yes. Isn't it funny I thought it was—no you're right. I was a little—you know, the night I was here. [HENRY *smiles.*] In fact, I thought I remembered Miss Herries promising to give it to us for a wedding present. [*Crosses Down Right.*] But—I suppose she changed her mind after Phyllis spilled that gossip.

HENRY. I'll be glad to remind Miss Herries if you could suggest some tactful method.

PETER. [*Laughs. Crosses back Up Right.*] Never mind. Anyway it doesn't look as nice as it did the night I first saw it. The hell with it.

[*Snaps his fingers. Crosses Down Right. Doorbell rings.* MRS. EDWARDS *crosses toward the front door.*]

HENRY. I shall tell Miss Herries in my next letter that you called.

PETER. Do that. [*Reflects.*] No—you'd better not. The other half of the family have all decided not to—bother her—until she asks them to.

HENRY. I'm extremely sorry. [MRS. EDWARDS *brings in cable, hands to* HENRY, *who opens it.*] Excuse me.

[MRS. EDWARDS *leaves out Left.* HENRY, *crossing to Left Center reads cable without any sign of emotion, and puts it in his pocket.*]

PETER. [*Crosses to desk—puts out cigarette.*] Well, I'm off. My—wife and I are going to live in America, you know.

HENRY. Indeed.

PETER. [*Crosses to Center.*] I'm going to take charge of a branch out in Kansas City. Ever hear of it?

HENRY. Oh, yes.

PETER. God help me!

HENRY. Good luck, sir!

PETER. Thank you, sir! [*Crosses Up Center.*] Well, I'll tell the—family about Miss Herries—not that it matters much, I suppose.

HENRY. [*Follows* PETER.] I shall be here until Miss Herries returns and I'll be glad to do anything I can—

PETER. [*Laughs.*] That's all right. Goodbye.

[HENRY *sees* PETER *out.* MR. *and* MRS. EDWARDS *come on and wait until* HENRY *returns. They enter from dining room.* MR. EDWARDS *goes up on platform.* MRS. EDWARDS *goes to above table Left.* HENRY *re-enters, still fingering the cablegram. He looks at them a bit triumphantly.*]

MR. EDWARDS. [*As* HENRY *enters.*] Nicely done, Henry.

HENRY. [*Crossing to window to watch* PETER *leave.*] Yes, I think so. [*Then, handing cable to* EDWARDS. *Crossing to Right Center.*] This is interesting.

[EDWARDS *reads.* HENRY *sits at desk.*]

MRS. EDWARDS. [*Crossing a bit Right.*] What is it, Father?

MR. EDWARDS. Feller named Weston cables that his wife, Lucy, was killed in an airplane crash near Marseilles.

MRS. EDWARDS. My goodness—

[MR. EDWARDS *hands cable back to* HENRY.]

HENRY. That settles it. I think that when Miss Herries hears of *this*, things will be much simpler. [*Pause.*] It also adds a note of permanency to the whole venture. For now, Miss Herries has no one but me. [*Bell.*] That should be Rosenberg. [*Crosses to window and looks out. Then to* EDWARDS.] Let her come down. I want her to meet this chap.

MRS. EDWARDS. Oh, Henry—

HENRY. I'll go out through the basement and come around and let myself in—in a few minutes. Show the man in here. Then you let Miss Herries into this room. Listen carefully. Don't let the man get away if she starts anything. [HENRY *rearranges things on desk.*]

MRS. EDWARDS. [*A little fearfully.*] Who is it, Henry?

MR. EDWARDS. It's a dealer from Paris.

[*Nodding that it's all right. Doorbell.*]

HENRY. [*Crossing to dining room door Left.*] Go on. [MR. EDWARDS *goes upstairs.* MRS. EDWARDS *again waits until he has gone up. She looks back at* HENRY *as if a little afraid of this step.*] All right.

[*Reassuringly.* MRS. EDWARDS *goes to the door.* HENRY *lingers until he hears* ROSENBERG'S *voice, then goes out through the door Up Left.*]

MRS. EDWARDS. [*Off.*] Yes, sir?

MR. ROSENBERG. [*Off.*] Monsieur Henry Abbott.

MRS. EDWARDS. [*Off.*] Yes, sir.

MR. ROSENBERG. [*Off.*] Monsieur Gustav Rosenberg, Bernstein et Fils. My card.

MRS. EDWARDS. [*Off.*] Come in, sir. [*Shows in* MR. ROSENBERG, *a Frenchman.*] Mr. Abbott is expected. Will you wait here, sir.

MR. ROSENBERG. Thank you.

[MR. ROSENBERG *looks around the room, spots the Whistler and comes down to it, putting his hat on table Left.* MRS. EDWARDS *backs out Right. He glances at the windows and sees the shutters and realizes that he cannot get more natural light—examines the canvas—front and back. He takes out his handkerchief, spits on it, and rubs the lower Right, then the lower Left corner of the canvas. He does not find any trace of a signature —which doesn't bother him particularly, however. What does disturb him is the fact that his handkerchief is black with dirt. He is putting his handkerchief back in his pocket, and sitting in Left chair as* MARY HERRIES *enters the room from the stairs.*]

MARY. [*Stops on platform—sees* MRS. EDWARDS *off Right then looks into room Center—on platform.*] Who—who are you?

[*She knows that the* EDWARDS' *are listening and that, she must play the part she is expected to play. This man, however, is a perfect stranger—he may be one of* HENRY'S *satellites—this may be another trap.*]

MR. ROSENBERG. [*Rising.*] Good afternoon, Madame. I am M. Gustav Rosenberg, Bernstein et Fils.

MARY. [*Crossing Down Center.*] What are you doing here?

MR. ROSENBERG. [*A little puzzled.*] I—I am M. Gustav Rosenberg. M. Abbott has invited me to look at this painting.

MARY. Painting?

MR. ROSENBERG. Yes—this painting—this Whistler.

MARY. [*Crossing in front of Left Center chair. Hurt.*] No! Oh.

MR. ROSENBERG. What is it, Madame; are you ill?

MARY. Oh, no. I'm quite all right. Only sometimes—I forget. [*She must make sure who he is.*] I've even forgotten who you said you were.

MR. ROSENBERG. [*Now beginning to worry.*] M. Rosenberg, Madame. Bernstein et Fils, Paris.

MARY. Oh, yes. But are you *really?* [*Suddenly, with more intensity.*] How do I know you are M. Rosenberg, from Paris?

MR. ROSENBERG. [*Presenting business card.*] My card, Madame.

MARY. [*This is not enough identification.*] No!

MR. ROSENBERG. My passport. [*Shows it to her.*]

MARY. [MARY *looks at it quickly, realizes that here may be a friend. Then she senses that the others are listening and speaks for their benefit.*] Oh. Well, it doesn't make any difference. You'll forget me. *Everybody's forgotten me. I'm supposed to be away.* Henry writes all my letters.

ROSENBERG. [*A bit puzzled.*] Pardon, Madame?

MARY. *No one else sees me.* [*She takes a letter from her dress.*] How do you like that picture? [*Points to* HENRY'S *painting of the "Ranz Des Vaches" on Left wall.*]

MR. ROSENBERG. That? Oh, yes—yes—yes.

MARY. [*Points at letter which she has taken out of her dress.*] *Please look at this!* [*Then for the benefit of the others.*] It's Henry's picture. [*Puts the letter in his pocket.*] Henry Abbott did it all. *Do you see?*

MR. ROSENBERG. I—I don't know— [*Reaches into his pocket.*] Madame,—what is *this?*

MARY. [*Pulls his hand away from his pocket.*] The cowherd is playing the flute. And the cows are listening. [*Points to the arch.*] *They're listening very carefully, do you see?*

MR. ROSENBERG. Yes—to be sure –

MARY. [*Points to his pocket.*] *You must look at it.*

MR. ROSENBERG. Oh—yes—yes, of course—

MARY. Henry isn't a very good painter. [*Low and pleading for* ROSENBERG *to believe her.*] *He's the very worst sort*— [*Her voice rises so the others may hear.*] of a painter.

MR. ROSENBERG. Yes—yes, indeed! [*He looks around, hoping someone will enter.*]

MARY. [*Pointing to letter.*] *I'd tell that to anyone*— even to *Lucy Weston*—who lives in *Mentone*—*Mentone*— [*Then for the benefit of the others.*] But she's too far away. Do you agree with me?

MR. ROSENBERG. Yes, Madame—yes. [*Anything to quiet her.*] Please sit down.

MARY. [*Sits quietly in Left Center chair.*] Are you going to wait for Mr. Abbott? Or— [*Rises and draws* ROSENBERG *up Center.*] Will you *go away now* and come back later?

MR. ROSENBERG. I was told to wait here, Madame.

MARY. You could come back later.

MR. ROSENBERG. I am sorry, Madame. I have other appointments. I am in London for a few hours only. Please sit down, Madame.

[MARY *sits in chair Right Center.*]

MARY. But you will remember what I've said about— [*Pointing to letter in his pocket.*] the picture?

ROSENBERG. Yes, Madame.

[*The front door is heard closing.*]

MARY. Please—help me—*do something!*

[ROSENBERG *crosses Up Center.* HENRY ABBOTT *enters the room.*]

HENRY. Mr. Rosenberg! [*Shaking hands.*]

MR. ROSENBERG. Ah! Mr. Abbott!

HENRY. You've had a look at the Whistler, I suppose?

MR. ROSENBERG. Yes—I—I have. I am glad you are here.

HENRY. [*Sees that everything has gone as planned. Crosses to fireplace.*] Yes. [*Crosses to the Whistler.*] Well—what do you think of it?

MR. ROSENBERG. [*Crosses after* HENRY. MARY *gives* ROSENBERG *a look of pleading.*] Oh, yes—yes.

HENRY. Do you think Bernstein et Fils will be interested?

[*All through this,* MARY *is sitting quietly without making a move, watching* MR. ROSENBERG *with desperate hope.*]

MR. ROSENBERG. [*A bit distracted by* MARY, *forces himself to discuss the picture.*] As I have told you, M. Abbott, Bernstein et Fils are not interested in Whistler —except for this one client.

HENRY. Yes, of course.

MR. ROSENBERG. Like so many Whistlers, it has sunken in and darkened to an extraordinary degree.

HENRY. Undoubtedly a good cleaning and one coat of mastic will bring out any details—

MR. ROSENBERG. Of course—this light— [*He shrugs, turns Right sees* MARY, *turns back to* HENRY, *picks up hat.*] Might I suggest that you have it sent to our London correspondent—Leicester Galleries, Leicester Square for further examination.

HENRY. Oh, it's genuine, all right.

MR. ROSENBERG. Of course. You will also accompany the painting with the history and the letter of authenticity.

HENRY. Oh, yes.

[MARY *looks pleadingly at* ROSENBERG.]

ROSENBERG. Au 'voir, M'sieur. [*Crosses up between Left Center chair and table.*]

HENRY. Good day, Mr. Rosenberg.

MR. ROSENBERG. [*Crosses up to Arch, stops, turns back.*] Ah—uh—Mr. Abbott—

HENRY. [*Goes to him.*] Yes?

MR. ROSENBERG. The lady gave me this. [*Produces letter.*] Perhaps it would be better—

HENRY. Oh, yes. Thank you for understanding.

MR. ROSENBERG. Au 'voir, M'sieur Abbott.

HENRY. Au 'voir.

[MR. ROSENBERG *goes.* HENRY *follows him off.* MR. ED-
WARDS *enters to below table Left.* MRS. EDWARDS *to
above Left Center chair.* ADA *to in front of fireplace.*]

MR. EDWARDS. Well!

HENRY. [*Re-enters—nods—a close call—then gives letter to* MARY.] Here's your letter.

MARY. [*Low—with despair, still sitting Right Center.*]
God!

MR. EDWARDS. From listening, I'd have sworn she
was—

HENRY. You are to be complimented. Miss Herries.
[*Then to* MRS. EDWARDS, *crossing to below Left Center
chair.*] Take her upstairs.

MARY. [*Gets up and faces* HENRY, *firmly, resolutely and
with as much strength as she can muster. She speaks
evenly and quietly.*] Don't be too sure, Henry Abbott. Things end somehow—sometime— Someone—
It's been too easy for you. How you must despise your-
selves! [*Almost a whisper.*] You wretched people—
[*There is a pause.* MARY *starts upstairs.* MRS. EDWARDS
offers to help, but MARY *draws away. Then as* MARY
goes up the stairs—

FADE OUT

EPILOGUE

Scene: The lights dim up and we find the scene as it was at the end of the Prologue. MARY *is seated Left Center—and* MR. FOSTER *is seated Right Center.*

MR. FOSTER. [*Greatly agitated.*] Good God—I beg your pardon, Miss Herries—but I mean—

MARY. You do believe me, don't you?

MR. FOSTER. Miss Herries! Really, I—I—I—

MARY. The rain has stopped. Henry will soon be here.

MR. FOSTER. [*Rising and pacing.*] This is dreadful—dreadful. What's to be done?

MARY. [*Hands him note.*] Please take this. Take it.

[FOSTER *looks at the note—then doorslam—*FOSTER *hurriedly puts away note.* HENRY *enters and sees* FOSTER.]

HENRY. Hello, Foster. You waited, thank you. I'm sorry to be late. [*He turns on lights and then notices* MARY.] Oh, Aunt Mary! [*He crosses to her.*] Down for your tea, dear?

MARY. Yes.

HENRY. Where is it?

MARY. No one was here.

HENRY. No one here? I don't understand. [*Crosses and rings bell, then crosses to desk.*] Now, Mr. Foster. You want me to sign these papers, don't you?

MR. FOSTER. The signature required by the Inland Revenue.

HENRY. Fine. Where do I sign, Mr. Foster?

MR. FOSTER. Here, sir. This will clear your income tax through June of this year.

HENRY. Till June. [*He starts signing.*]

MR. EDWARDS. [*Who has entered and put coffee table in front of* MARY. EDWARDS *is in the uniform of the traditional butler.*] You rang, sir?

HENRY. [*Crosses to* MARY *with a protective air.*] Yes, Edwards. I will not have you all away from the house at the same time. Miss Herries should never be without someone at her call. I've told you that before.

MR. EDWARDS. We are very sorry, sir, but the rain held us up. I had to take Mrs. Edwards to the doctor. She's not feeling well, sir. And we thought—

HENRY. I want it definitely understood that Miss Herries is not to be left alone at any time. You were engaged to attend to Miss Herries' wants at all hours. If that isn't plain I shall have to get someone who will. Make it clear to Mrs. Edwards. And we'll have tea now.

MR. EDWARDS. Yes, sir. Mrs. Edwards is preparing it.

[*He goes toward dining room—stands aside so* MRS.

EDWARDS *can come in with tea tray, which she places on coffee table before* MARY. MR. EDWARDS *exits.* HENRY *has gone back to desk, immediately.*]

HENRY. Now, then, Mr. Foster. Sorry. [*Resumes signing Income Tax blanks.*]

FOSTER. That's all right, sir.

MRS. EDWARDS. [*After she has placed tea in front of* MARY—*crosses to Center.*] I'm sorry about being out, Mr. Abbott.

HENRY. All right, Mrs. Edwards. [*He finishes signing —to* FOSTER. MRS. EDWARDS *exits Left on platform.*] Thank you, Mr. Foster.

FOSTER. [*Picks up papers and puts them in his envelope.*] Not at all. [*Crosses down to* MARY.] Good day, Madam.

MARY. Oh, you're leaving? Good day, then.

FOSTER. [*Turns to* HENRY *who has risen and is at Right of desk.*] Good day, Mr. Abbott.

HENRY. Good day, Mr. Foster. [MR. FOSTER *starts out Up Center.* HENRY *lets him go almost out, then stops him.*] Mr. Foster. [FOSTER *stops—looks at* HENRY— *then slowly comes back into room to* HENRY *in front of desk.*] You've never been here before, have you?

FOSTER. No, sir.

HENRY. I'm sorry there was no one here.

MR. FOSTER. [*After a moment.*] Oh—I understand. Mr. Abbott.

[ADA, *in the costume of a trained nurse comes downstairs.*]

HENRY. I thought you might not know.

MR. FOSTER. That's quite all right, sir. [*He sees* ADA *arranging* MARY'S *shawl*—ADA *exits Left.*] She had me going for a few moments, Mr. Abbott.

[MARY *registers despair.*]

HENRY. Ah, yes. [*He crosses to* MARY—FOSTER *starts out Up Center.* HENRY *stops him.*] Mr. Foster, my aunt is sometimes left alone—as she was today. Carelessness on the part of the servants. [*Then a deliberate statement—not a question.*] She gave you something— a note. [*He holds out his hand.*]

MR. FOSTER. Oh! [*This is an ambiguous "oh"—and there is life and death in the balance. A look passes between* FOSTER *and* MARY.] No, sir! Good day, Mr. Abbott.

[*He exits. The door slams after* FOSTER *is heard.* HENRY *slowly turns and crosses to* MARY *and stands looking at her. After a moment* MR. EDWARDS *enters from dining room. Crosses to Upper Center on platform. He, too, is puzzled and nervous. With his head he beckons* MRS. EDWARDS *on from Left. She joins* MR. EDWARDS *and both look at* MARY. *When* MRS. EDWARDS *has joined* MR. EDWARDS, ADA *is heard running down the stairs. She stops at* MR. EDWARDS' *right, frightened. She slowly goes to the Right side of the arch. Then* MR. EDWARDS *comes down behind* MARY. *He looks at* MARY, *then at* HENRY.]

MR. EDWARDS. What do you think, Henry?

[HENRY *does not answer. He is still watching* MARY. MR. EDWARDS *starts toward the upper window. Just before he reaches the window—doorbell.* MR. EDWARDS *hurries to upper window, followed by* ADA *and* MRS. EDWARDS. HENRY *hurries to downstage window. They all look out. The doorbell rings, and knocking. Slowly the* EDWARDS *and* HENRY *straighten up and look at each other—then at* MARY. *Doorbell and knocking again.* MARY *slowly rises from her chair. She seems to grow in stature. She throws off her shawl.*]

MARY. I'll answer.—

CURTAIN

[*On the curtain* MARY *is crossing Up Center to go out. The doorbell is ringing and the knocking is louder and more commanding.*]

PROPERTY PLOT

SET PROPS

RIGHT WALL

Heavy drapes and lace curtains on windows

REAR WALL

In Upper Right corner—small table

Chest Upper Right under panel

Table Upper Left next to arch

Chest Upper Left under panel

LEFT WALL

Vases on brackets—one each side of mantel

Fire grate in fireplace

Fire guard, and set of fire-irons

STAGE LEFT

Small upholstered bench in front of fireplace

Two large upholstered chairs with table between

STAGE RIGHT

Sofa

Desk

Coffee table

2 side chairs

(For arrangements—see plans)

BAY WINDOW

Drapes and lace curtains on windows

Large chest

One plant in front of each window on stand.

CARPET COVERS COMPLETE STAGE, PLATFORMS, AND
   STAIRS.

HAND AND TRIM PROPS

ACT ONE, SCENE 1

ON STAGE
  On Mantel
    Clock and two china dogs
  On Table Left
    Table runner, cigarette box, ashtray, matches, 2
      magazines, jade cigarette case, several wrapped
      Xmas packages, envelope.
  On Chest Upper Left
    Runner, china bowl with red flowers, statue of
      horse, books.
  On Table Upper Left
    Lamp, books, magazine
  On Chest Upper Right
    Table runner
  On Table Upper Right Corner
    Lamps, books, magazines.
  On Desk
    Large blotter, pen-and-ink set, hand blotter, pad
      of scratch paper, check book, letter opener, tele-
      phone, cigarette box, matches, 2 ashtrays.
  Coffee Table
    Cigarette box, matches, ashtray.
  Chest in Bay Window
    2 ornamental figures, Siamese Buddha, small Xmas
      tree.

On Chair Left Center
    Woman's open over-night case, a few wrapped
        presents in it.
OFF RIGHT
    Xmas present, for Peter
    Money, for Mary
OFF LEFT [*dining room*]
    Piece of red ribbon
    Tray with siphon, decanter, 2 glasses
    Plate of sandwiches on tray
OFF LEFT [*upstairs*]
    Coat, for Mary

ACT ONE, SCENE 2

STRIKE OFF
    Xmas tree
    Tray with siphon and decanter
    Flowers from bowl
ON STAGE
    Brandy decanter on table
    Statue (Troubetskoi) on Table Left
OFF RIGHT
    2 paintings, for Henry
    2 Napoleon brandy glasses, Peter and Phyllis
    Coat, for Rose
    Baby, for Rose
OFF LEFT [*upstairs*]
    Small present, for Mary
    Smelling salts, for Rose

ACT TWO

STRIKE OFF
  Brandy decanter and glass
  Shoes left by Ada
  Paintings left by Henry
ON STAGE
  Phone books on desk
  Wastepaper basket under desk
  (HENRY *to have key and money*)
OFF LEFT [*upstairs*]
  Baby, for Mrs. Edwards
OFF RIGHT
  Gramophone with hammer and nails and record in-
      side, for Mr. Edwards
    (Record used: "L'Augerge du Cheval Blanc" see
    "Sound Equipment")

ACT TIIREE

STRIKE OFF
  Gramophone
  Baby
  Hat
  Phone and phone books
  Horse statue
ON STAGE
  Shutters closed on windows
  Pan of potatoes and paring knife on desk
  Newspaper in Chair Left
  Statue (Troubetskoi) on Chest Upper Right

List of paintings on desk
Whistler painting standing in Upper Left Corner
Drapes and curtains wide open

OFF LEFT [*upstairs*]

Letter, for Mary

OFF LEFT [*downstairs*]

Pencil and paper, for Henry

OFF RIGHT

Several sealed letters, for Mrs. Edwards
Cablegram, for Mrs. Edwards
Fountain pen and blue covered document, for Henry
Attache case, for Henry
Card case, passport, magnifying glass, handkerchief,
    for Rosenberg

PROLOGUE AND EPILOGUE

STRIKE OFF

Whistler painting
Statue (Troubetskoi)
Papers on desk
Coffee Table

ON STAGE

Curtains draped together again

OFF LEFT [*dining room*]

Letter, for Mary
Coffee Table
Tea tray with cups, saucers, pot, cream and sugar,
    etc.
Three-shelved sandwich stand

OFF RIGHT

Umbrella and brown paper case (legal papers inside)

PICTURE ON SET

Act One, Scenes 1 & 2, and Act Two
Over Mantel—Long portrait (Whistler)
Over Left Door—Small landscape
Left side back wall—1 Whistler, 1 El Greco
Right side back wall—2 Whistlers
Center of Bay Window—Large portrait—man—
    18th Century
On wall above stairs—2 small, heavy-framed land-
    scapes
On wall going off Right to front door—Medium
    sized portrait man—18th Century
Act III
Over Mantel—Henry's "Ranz des Vaches"
Left side back wall—2 small modern paintings
Right side back wall—1 Whistler removed, other
    still there (All other pictures—stet)
Prologue and Epilogue
Right side back wall—modern portrait—woman
    (All other pictures as in Act III)

SOUND EQUIPMENT

Amplifying Equipment
1—10 watt amplifier
1—two-turntable pickup with separate faders on each
    pickup
1—mixing panel
    1—variable scratch filter
    1—variable tone control
1—master fader for turntables

1—large speaker Upper Left behind scenery
2—large speakers—fastened to front of balcony.
boxes in auditorium
1—small speaker Down Right—used as pilot to hear
auditorium speaker when curtain is down
1—output distribution panel
Cut-off switch, pilot light, and fader for auditorium speakers
Cut-off switch and pilot light for Upper Left
speaker
Fader for pilot speaker
1—DC-AC converter in basement
Necessary cable, connectors, etc.

GRAMOPHONE RECORDS USED
"L'Auberge du Cheval Blanc"—Columbia #DF982
—Mazurka
"The Isle of the Dead"—Victor #7220B—Part 4
Chimes—Victor #V-6199B
Chimes—"Oh, Come All Ye Faithful" Harmony
#78002

DOORSLAM—off stage Upper Right
DOORKNOCKER—off stage Upper Right
RAIN—off Right [*an electrically driven rain drum was
used*]
TELEPHONE BELL—Right between windows
DOORBELL—off Upper Left

SOUND PLOT

(NOTE: for doorbell and telephone cues, see "Stage
Manager's Cues")
FROM PROLOGUE TO ACT ONE
As the stage darkens and after curtain is down, "The

Isle of the Dead" is heard over the auditorium speakers. After a few bars of this "L'Augerge du Cheval Blanc" is mixed in slowly until it predominates and then fades out leaving "Isle of the Dead," which in turn fades just before the curtain rises on Act One.

END OF ACT ONE, Scene one.

Harmony Chimes "Oh, Come All Ye Faithful" is heard alone until about two notes beyond the first phrase, then Victor Chimes (pealing bells) is added. Both are cut as curtain strikes the floor. Upper Left offstage speaker is heard.

FROM ACT THREE TO EPILOGUE

The same records, same speakers and same sequence used as from Prologue to Act One.

SIGNAL RUNS

Telephone bell, operated from Stage Manager's desk —Down Right

Doorbell, operated from Stage manager's desk— Down Right

Entrance signal lights:

1—off Left to cue stairs and Left entrances

1—off Right to cue entrances and doorslams

STAGE MANAGER'S CUES

PROLOGUE

Page

P–1—Doorbell—3 times (At rise)
P–1—Doorslam

ACT ONE, SCENE I

1–1–2—Doorbell "That's hard to say, Mrs. *Weston*"
1–1–5—Telephone ". . . miles of driving to *do.*"
1–1–6 —Doorslam—Before Mary and Henry enter
1–1–11—Doorbell "I'll eat them outside" *XXXX*
1–1–16—Entrance Left—Henry Crosses back to Right
       after putting case in pocket
1–1–18—Doorslam—Henry's exit
1–1–18—Entrance Left—Mary goes to Upper Left
       Chest
1–1–19—Chimes—"Goodnight"

ACT ONE, SCENE II

1–2–29—Doorbell "statue for a wedding present"
       XXXX
1–2–32—Doorslam "old man to bless you"

ACT TWO

2–1—Doorbell (At rise)
2–1—Doorslam—Edwards' entrance

2–7—Doorbell—(2 times) Edwards going upstairs
2–11—Doorbell—"very old and helpless"
2–13—Doorslam—"Have a nice trip, Lucy"
2–18—Lights—Dim

ACT THREE

3–1—Doorbell and knocks—After Mary bus. Mr. Edwards reading
3–1—Doorslam—After letter business—Mr. Edwards resumes reading
3–8—Doorbell—"Steady employment"
3–16—Doorbell—"The hell with it!"
3–17—Doorslam—"That's all right. Goodbye"
3–18—Doorbell—"Miss Herries has no one but me" *XXXX*
3–18—Doorbell—"It's a dealer from Paris"
3–19—Signal Left Rosenberg starts to put picture back
3–22—Doorslam—"Yes, Madame"
3–24—Doorslam—Rosenberg's exit

EPILOGUE

E–1—Doorslam—"Please take this. Take it." Foster looks at note
E–1—Lights—Henry switches on lights
E–4—Doorslam—Foster's exit
E–5—Doorbell—Edwards crosses to above desk on way to window
E–5—Doorbell and knocker—All are looking out window
E–5—Doorbell and knocker—They straighten up
E–5—Doorbell and knocker "I'll answer it" *XXXX*

LIGHTING EQUIPMENT CARRIED

4—500 watt Lekolites with color frames

23—1000 watt spotlights with color frames

2—500 watt spotlights with color frames

1—400 watt spotlight with color frame

4—sections compartment footlights—color frames

2—6 light Frink reflector borderlights—color frames

2—6 light borderlights—color frames—500 watt

4—10″ projectors and color frames

4—16″ projectors with color frames

1—Olivette with color frame, on stand

22—4-way cutoffs

1—6-way plugging box

17—4-way plugging box

1—asbestos cloth

1—10′ stand

2—18′ stands with heavy base and ring in top

1—34′ pipe batten

3—20′ pipe battens

2—30′ pipe battens

1—Fire grate

1—Chandelier

2—wall brackets

2—table lamps

2—switchboards with cable leads

Also necessary cable and connectors and hanging arms

LAMPS

   62—50 watt A type
    1—400 watt G30
    1—500 watt G30
    1—500 watt G40
   12—500 watt PS
    4—500 watt T12
   12—200 watt PS
    1—1000 watt PS
   31—1000 watt G40

Gelatines used (Century)

   #3 Flesh Pink
   #57 Light Amber
   #62 Light Scarlet
   #29 Special Steel Blue
   #69 Special Chocolate

LIGHTING SET UP

IN BOOTH

   4 Lekolites—2 amber, 2 blue, covering full stage

FOOTS

   4 sections—amber, pink, and blue

BORDER PIPE (numbering from Stage Right to Left)

   1. 1000 w—amber—sofa
   2. 1000 w—pink—sofa
   3. 1000 w—amber—Right Center
   One section border lights—blue, amber, pink—
     200 w.
   4. 1000 w—blue—Right Center
   5. 1000 w—amber—sofa

6. 1000 w—blue—Center
7. 1000 w—blue—Left Center
8. 1000 w—amber—Left Center Chair

One section border lights—blue, amber, pink—
200 w.

9. 1000 w—amber—Left Chair
10. 1000 w—pink—Left Center Chair
11. 1000 w—pink—Upper Left Center
12. 1000 w—amber—Left Chair

OFF STAGE LEFT

500 w—amber—dining room door

OFF STAGE RIGHT

(2 pipes run Up and Down stage)

Covering down stage windows:

2—16″ projectors—blue and chocolate—1000 w.
1—1000 w spotlight—amber—through opening in
shutter

Covering Up stage window:

(same as downstage)

Two 6-light, 500 w. border lights, amber, blue, to
light cyc.

One Olivette on stand to light Down stage window—
amber

IN HALLWAY RIGHT

1—1000 w spotlight—Scarlet
1—1000 w spotlight—Pink

IN HALLWAY LEFT

1—1000 w spotlight—Pink
1—1000 w spotlight—Scarlet

BAY WINDOW RIGHT

2—10″ projectors—amber
1—Olivette on stand—blue

Bay Window Left
   2—10″ projectors—amber
   1—1000 w spotlight—blue

SWITCHBOARD READINGS

(approximate)

Prologue
   Blue window projectors—⅓ **up**
   Hall spots ½
   Blue cross ray—Full
   Blue spots—¾ up
   Amber & Pink spots—⅛ **up**
   Blue booth spots—¾ up
      (Dim out at end of scene)
Act One, Scene 1
      (Dim up at start of scene)
   Hall spotlights about ¾ up
   All other spots a little over ½ Foots added—no blue
      cross ray
   No outside lights
   Table lamps on.
      (Dim out booth spots as curtain comes down)
Act One, Scene 2
      (Dim up booth spots with curtain)
   Add in Chandelier and bracket lights
   Add in blue cross rays—full
   Pink and Amber cross rays up to about ¾
      (Dim out booth spots on curtain
      Dim out foots as house lights come up)
Act Two
   Window and cyc lights—Blue and amber about ½,
      Chocolate Full

Hall spots—¾ up

Blue cross rays and spots—⅓

Booth spots—¾ up

Foots, amber and pink spots and cross ray—⅓

(On cue—Dim)

Chocolate and amber window and cyc lights—out

Hall spots to under ½

Amber cross rays—out

Booth spots to ¼ up

Foots down 1 point

ACT THREE

Spotlights through shutters and Blue cross rays—
Full

Hall, Amber booth, Amber and pink spots, foots
about ⅛ up

Blue Spots and fronts lights—¾ up

Amber and pink cross rays—¼ up

(Dim out at end of act)

EPILOGUE

(Dim up to start scene)

Blue cross rays, spots, and booth—¾ up

Blue window lights—½ up

(On Cue)

Table lamps and amber fronts—¾ up

(Then slowly bring in hall spots, and generally
warm up the whole scene by adding in Amber
and Pink spots to ¼)

COSTUME PLOT

  Mary Herries   —gray crepe negligee
                      white wool shawl
                      gray mules
  Maid   —old gray house dress
                      old white apron
                      black shoes
                      black cotton hose
  Mr. Foster   —black overcoat
                      black bowler hat
                      morning coat
                      striped trousers
                      black shoes

Act One, Scene 1
  Mary Herries   —short sable cape
                      rose taffeta evening gown
                      long pearl gray gloves
                      rose crepe slippers
  Lucy Weston   —green crepe evening gown
                      green net jacket
                      green crepe slippers
  Rose   —black crepe dress
                      white net collars, cuffs, apron, cap
                      black pumps
                      silk hose
  Henry   —old brown trousers

old dark blue coat
old dark blue longshoreman's jer-
sey
old shoes
old hat

Phyllis   —Brown Harris tweed coat
yellow crepe evening gown

Peter   —Black overcoat
white muffler
dress suit

Act One, Scene 2

Mary Herries —·green crepe hostess gown
green crepe slippers

Phyllis   —pink moire evening gown
pink moire slippers

Peter   —dress suit

Henry   —same trousers
same coat
dirty white shirt and tie

Doctor   —dark overcoat
dark gray suit
black shoes
dark felt hat

Ada   —green furred coat
blue wool skirt
tan sweater
cheap black silk hose
cheap black patent leather shoes

Act Two

Mary Herries —lavender chiffon tea gown
lavender crepe slippers

                          navy blue kid shoes
                          light blue silk crepe blouse
                          navy blue felt hat
                          navy blue cotton gloves
                          navy blue cheap bag
Henry   —dark blue double breasted suit
                          dark tie, shoes and socks
Doctor   —(same)

ACT THREE
Mary Herries   —black velvet negligée
                          black slippers
Henry   —morning coat (double breasted)
                          light gray trousers
                          spats
                          stiff turn up collar
                          dark tie
Ada   —Same as Act I—(no coat)
Mrs. Edwards   —maid's black sateen uniform
                          white organdie collar, cuffs
                          black shoes and hose
                          kitchen apron
Mr. Rosenberg   —full length morning coat
                          striped trousers
                          dark vest
                          dark tie
                          black fedora
Mr. Edwards   —dark coat
                          striped trousers
                          Stand up collar
                          dark tie

EPILOGUE
Mary Herries   —(Same as Prologue)

Mr. Foster —(Same as Prologue)

Henry —cutaway
same trousers as Act III
spats
gray ascot tie

Mrs. Edwards —Same as Act III
with maid's white apron and cap

Mr. Edwards —cutaway coat
striped trousers
white dickey
black straight tie
black vest

Ada —English nurse's costume
Medium blue chambray dress with high neck. Long sleeves. Full gored skirt. Stiff white collar and cuffs with pearl studs. Full white apron with bib fitting under collar and with straps which cross in back. Wide starched belt with stud in front. Coif of stiffly starched linen Black hose and shoes.

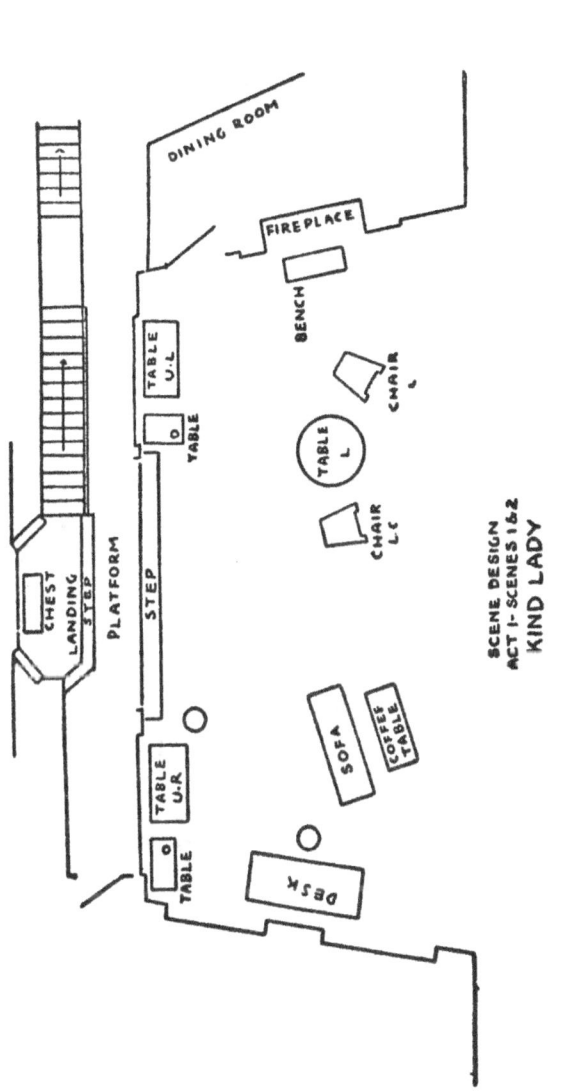

SCENE DESIGN
ACT I – SCENES 1 & 2
KIND LADY

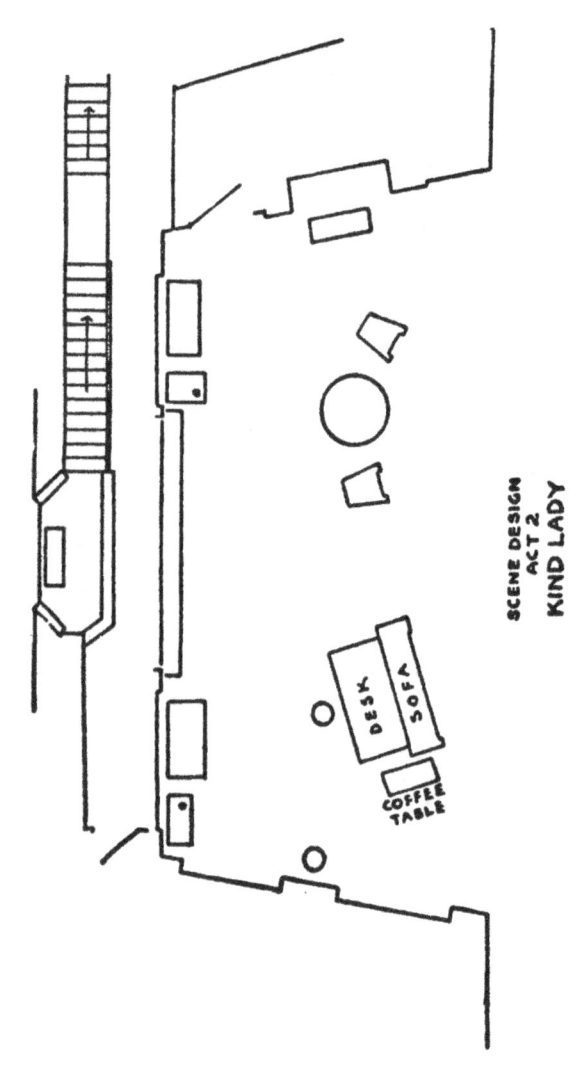

SCENE DESIGN
ACT 2
KIND LADY

DESK

SOFA

COFFEE
TABLE

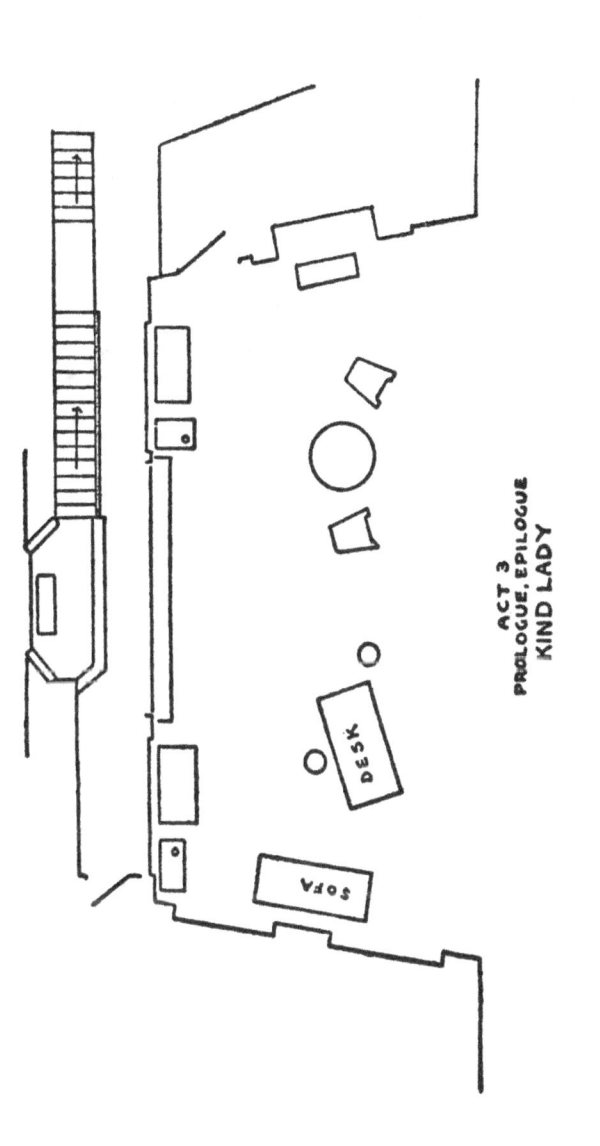

ACT 3
PROLOGUE, EPILOGUE
KIND LADY

MUSIC USE NOTE

Licensees are solely responsible for obtaining formal written permission from copyright owners to use copyrighted music in the performance of this play and are strongly cautioned to do so. If no such permission is obtained by the licensee, then the licensee must use only original music that the licensee owns and controls. Licensees are solely responsible and liable for all music clearances and shall indemnify the copyright owners of the play(s) and their licensing agent, Samuel French, against any costs, expenses, losses and liabilities arising from the use of music by licensees. Please contact the appropriate music licensing authority in your territory for the rights to any incidental music.

IMPORTANT BILLING AND CREDIT REQUIREMENTS

If you have obtained performance rights to this title, please refer to your licensing agreement for important billing and credit requirements.